Pulp Modern

Hand of Doom Fall 2025

Clifford Ball

I0619287

Sarah Cannavo

J.D. Graves

H.P. Lovecraft

Anthony Perconti

E.F. Sweetman

Edited by Alec Cizak

Uncle B. Publications, LLC

Pulp Modern Fall 2025: Hand of Doom
Published and produced by
Uncle B. Publications, LLC and Larque Press LLC
Pulp Modern is funded in part by Yuan Sang.

Chief Editor: Alec Cizak
Design: Richard Krauss and Alec Cizak
All incidental artwork: Allen Koszowski
Adaptation illustrations and cover art: Ann Hoekstra.

Printed in the United States of America and other countries.

Contact information for Uncle B. Publications, LLC may be obtained through
the website: unclebpublications.com

Contact information for Larque Press LLC may be obtained through the
website: larquepress.com

ISBN-978-1-957034-27-0

CONTENTS

Three Locations!

11 E. Market Street
(317) 237-0397

7301 W. 10th Street
(317) 271-7610

5767 E. 86th Street
(317) 845-9991

From the Editor

Alec Cizak

Work sucks. We all know it. Our time on this mortal coil is dreadfully short. In effort to put food on the table and a roof overhead, we're asked to sacrifice anywhere from eight to twelve to sometimes more hours a day for the profit of someone else. We get a pittance once or twice a month. We fork that brief fortune over for said room and board. Then we do it all over again. Never getting ahead. Never getting to a spot where we're no longer beholden to anyone but ourselves. When we're old, if we're lucky, we have a granted pittance we survive off until they toss us into the dirt to provide yet more of ourselves for separate entities.

Depressing. I know. Things have always been this way. Power rests in the hands of the few. That power is sustained by the labor of the many. Alleged thinkers have proposed solutions over the centuries. None have been particularly successful. The more utopian ideals lead only to mass murder. And capitalism, the best plan laid out on paper, collapses in the clutches of greed.

We have no system for human happiness. We have band-aids, like religion. Like drugs. Like sex. But no viable solution has ever been presented to save the working class from the hand of doom. A hand conjured centuries ago. A hand that refuses to loosen its grip.

So, what do you do?

You can complain.
You can cry.
You can scream.
Or you can laugh.

Pulp Modern's prescription is to scream until you laugh. Why not? The great stoics have always maintained you have no say in your mortality. You know not what happens after you shuffle off this mortal coil. Why burden yourself with worry?

Laugh.

In 2024, we dosed the audience with *Die Laughing*. Now we present the sequel, *Hand of Doom*. A batch of short stories containing both creatures of the night and exercises in empathy with those condemned to punch a clock for a paycheck. Our carousel of creatures includes vicious badgers, werewolves, mutated frogs, and zombies, among others. Our protagonists negotiate their fates to the best of their abilities. Because we are in the arena of horror, it's safe to say their struggles are noble, but ultimately futile.

Kind of like life.

So…laugh.

What else can you do?

This issue is filled with fiction by some of our very favorite writers and artists. We have *Pulp Modern* alums Sarah Cannavo and E.F. Sweetman. Two of the most reliable writers working in genre fiction today. We have a pair of stories by Texas legend J.D. Graves. A duo of classic pulp fiction yarns round out the literature portion of the magazine. Our resident pulp culture expert, Anthony Perconti provides a review of a classic monster mash up. Additionally, we'll have chats with our favorite Heavy Metal band, Thelemite, and special effects wizard Matt Barrett. Richard Krauss and I handled the art direction while newcomer Ann Hoekstra provides our fantastic story illustrations. And for seasoning, we have incidental artwork by Allen K.

As always, enjoy.

Alec Cizak
August 2025

YOU'RE GOING TO COME. BUT YOU MAY NEVER LEAVE.
CAMP HAYEWOOD
5
FRIDAY THE 69TH
PURRFESSIONAL PICTURES PRESENTS
BUD GALLOWAY AMBER KELLEHAN
CHRIS OFFERMAN AUSTEN JAYE
ERIC ANDERSON CROSBY PIOLATTO
PRODUCED, SHOT & CUT BY ALEX MONTILLA
X NO ONE UNDER 17 ADMITTED
STARRING AMY LETCHER & ROB ZOPPO
DAVID RUBIN INTRODUCING ANNA BESS
SAM BLUM KATARINA JOY LOPEZ
WILL TODISCO MUSIC BY CHRIS RANIER
WRITTEN & DIRECTED BY ALEX MONTILLA
©MMXXV PURRFESSIONAL PICTURES

The beast moved. Another blur scurrying up the staircase—chitter, chitter, chitter.

Badger!

adapted by J.D. Graves
original screenplay by Barry Wilkinson

A colorful variety of animals live in the forest. Some are familiar to us. And the most dangerous of these four-legged fiends remains Meles meles, or the common European badger. To describe this stout and stocky little creature, with a smallish head and eyes blacker than a doll's eyes, as territorial excuses the pure havoc they wreak. Twenty years after the "Slaughter at Thetford Forest" and a home office declaration of emergency, no right-thinking citizen could have imagined the furry menace's killing spree continuing for this long.

And yet the very real danger remains.

Jenny Welby sat across the breakfast table from the worm—her husband—William. Eyes locked on her tablet, unbelieving what she read. William's muddy voice prattled a cautious, "Good morning honey."

"Fuck right off!" Jenny blurted. Unaware of her husband's hurt reaction. Too busy staring at the digital file photo of her lover, Leonard.

"Something amiss?" William timidly asked his wife.

"Leonard's dead," Jenny fought back tears as her finger lingered on the picture.

"No, not Leonard Muskie!" William sighed, matching her abruptness with tactical empathy.

"Leonard Muskie?" Jenny asked. Brow knitted. "As

if…?"

Long pause followed, pregnant with disdain and abject confusion by both man and wife.

Finally, William broke their shared silence, "As if—what?"

"Leonard Ross you imbecile." Jenny screwed her face into a snarl. "As if I would waste ten seconds grieving that loser Muskie."

William showed her his palms. "I thought you liked him."

"What are you insinuating?" Jenny rattled her jewelry in his direction.

"Nothing," William said—his face tight with worry. "What happened to Leonard Ross?"

Why does the modern badger kill indiscriminately? Simple, its curiosity is stronger than fear. At least, this is the prevailing theory as to why this once nocturnal prowler suddenly turned savage. Of course, other alternative theories persist including that of debunked covert Russian interference. MI-6 itself refuted claims that Moscow secretly turned the once docile burrower into a brutal killing machine. Biological warfare aside, more popular concerns involved rising water pollution, prevalence of microplastics, and/or the Church of England invoking certain demonologies. Whatever the real reason, knowing the facts remains crucial to one's survival. If a badger happens across your path, do not engage with the blood-thirsty beast, turn around and run.

"Found his body greased across the train tracks for nearly two kilometers." Jenny choked up—still trying to process her own confused grief. "Authorities identified him through dental records." Lump swallowed in her throat. "They found part of his jaw in a nearby ditch."

William said something else she didn't hear—too lost in her own memories. They (her and Leonard (Ross not Muskie)) had shared an afternoon delight just two days ago. Could still smell his musk on the work shirt she wore now. It aroused a longing for the man who was now no more. Her black heart mourned the facts. Like the cryptic knowledge she'd never again be bent over this very breakfast table by his rough and ready stud service. Her bottom lip quivered. After all, there was no one quite like her Leonard. But there were millions of men like her William. Her ball and chain's milquetoast visage blurred into focus. Eyebrows pitched in sympathy, like a dog begging for a treat. "What about his Labrador...what was it's name?"

"Scout," Jenny said under her breath—remembering the evenings spent with Leonard painting her toenails in creamy peanut butter. Tears welled in her eyes. Now there was no one left to lick them clean.

"Right," William said, pleased she'd rejoined the conversation. "Was Scout found?"

Jenny shook her head.

"Don't fret," William reasoned, "that could be a good sign."

Jenny saw red—like waking from a nap on a sunny day—her jaw clenched. She seethed, "You inhuman monster."

William's face fell. Sweat broke across his forehead. She could smell his fear.

Slower than a Christmas morning, Jenny rose to her feet. Quiet rage boiled.

"I didn't mean nothing by it," William's scared school boy challenged. "Just making conversation before you were off for the day. Th-tha-that's all."

Oh, how she wanted to bury her steel-toed boots deep in his weak-jawed skull.

"I was only meaning that," William continued as if his life depended on it, "if the dog were found then it could've been just a harmless train accident and not a—"

"What?" She knew it before he said it. "Not a badger attack?!"

William winced—cowering from her expectant strike. The pathetic worm wriggled—small and insignificant. His punishment wasn't worth the effort.

After a beat, no violence came—his eyes fluttered open.

The Department of Environ-ment, Food, and Rural Affairs (DEFRA) announced plans to combat the dreaded Bovine Tuberculosis, or bTB, in 2012. DEFRA wrongly believed the deadly bTB to be spread by badgers to cows and to people. This dreaded scourge formed the well-

known line of contamination, resulting in millions of dollars of lost livestock and bloated NHS overhead. We now know bTB was a hoax perpetrated by the Liberal Government of Gordon Brown to help funnel money into offshore accounts to pay for his affair with an Elvis impersonator named Ted. Approximately, a hundred thousand badgers were culled at a cost of forty-seven million pounds.

If it was worth the effort, she'd make him suffer. Oh, how Jenny wanted to take her trusty cudgel and cull this fool right here on the spot. Would his eyes go wide with fear? Would his sniveling pink tongue poke from his newly dead mouth?

A little grin curled her thin lips—meanness sizzled. The fool needed to suffer her wrath. At once two black streaks painted his eyes. It wasn't fair—like most things—that her sweet Leonard was now gone. William's button nose darkened to a bulbous black. Leonard was too good for this world. William's smooth cheeks paled into a furry white. Leonard's chiseled chin—rough with stubble— could break hearts and start fires. But the memory was doused by this cowering fluff of disappointment.

One swing is all it would take.

One swing to notch another kill on her handle.

One swing and the seven rings of hell greeted another dead badger.

And this badger's biggest crime—tolerating Jenny's cruel version of romantic love.

While Jenny didn't mind being the family's sole bread-winner, she still desired to come home to a real man. Not some sissified beta-male who kept her knickers clean and their children fed. You know—a complete fucking wanker. Whipping William into a full commitment of pervasive neo-feminism had been the most enjoyable part over the years. However, she hadn't expected him to stay whipped. The animal husbandry of her husband had been too guided—too out-standing. Now she loathed the thing she'd lovingly trained.

Jenny's hand twitched.

William flinched. Then quickly gathered an envelope

from the table. He held it like a shield between them. His voice cracked, "Th-th-this came for you today!"

Jenny paused.

Saw the letterhead.

Eyes darted over the return address.

Unbelieving, they darted once again.

Finally, Jenny thought, she'd get everything she'd always wanted.

Thanks to DEFRA's efforts, Badger culling had gone from a routine act of humane mercy, into a dire blood sport. Which naturally attracted private equity. Wildcatter platoons sprouted seemingly overnight. The badger economy boomed. Cull Officers were expected to be ready at a moment's notice. As Badger attacks increased in frequency, more employees were needed to handle the volume. Training for such jobs became minimal, and the lowered threshold for entry brought with it typical organizational growing pains. These all sub-sided when companies instituted a com-mission-based payment system. Cull Officers could not expect to avoid the bloodshed and continue

to collect a cheque. No, they must be as deadly as the adversary they sought. No pelt brought home meant no money. A pound of Badger flesh brought home twen-ty pounds sterling.

"Congratulations," William said with a slight tremor, as if suddenly cold. "I knew you could do it. I never lost faith in my bird."

"Don't call me that," Jenny frowned. "This is one of the greatest moments of my life and you want to ruin it with name calling, you Badger-scat?"

William bit his lip. He knew better than to say more. Jenny took her place at center stage and read the letter aloud:

"In honor of your continued success in meeting production quotas, yadda-yadda-yadda. We at the Home Office are proud to invite you to be-come our newest executive administrator."

Jenny felt warm allover. Especially, when she read the handwritten note from her handsome friend Bruce. "Can't wait to share an 'office' with the Queen of the Cudgel."

Jenny didn't share this post-script with William. Even her arbitrary cruelty owned hard boundaries. Physical violence was never withheld; however, she drew a hard line at emotional devastation. No need to step on William's bollocks when he was already heeling at her feet. Besides, divorce remained an option, and infidelity remained a valid cause. Legal proceedings cost a fortune. And if William could prove Jenny's dalliances, then he'd be entitled to half of her money. That was not how she was going to play this game. Why should he be granted half of her badger numbers without lifting a finger?

Her tone softened. "William, The promotion ceremony will be held this Thursday. Please have the children there so that they can see their mum achieve her dreams. Be good to set a positive example for once."

With that said she left for work.

If she'd known it would be their last time together, she'd have at least kissed him goodbye.

NEWSFLASH:

MASSACRE IN MAN-CHESTER 9AM October 19th 2025

Twenty out of twenty-nine St. Lawrence Primary students found dead on field trip to the Science and Industry Museum. The surviving nine students were queuing for the loo while their peers were slaughtered. Officials are hesitant to jump to conclusions regarding the matter, however Godfrey Butler janitor of the S & I Museum was quoted as saying, "I don't know what done it. But...the eviscerations look like badger work to me alright."

NEWSFLASH:

PANIC IN THE STREETS OF NORWICH 13:00 October 19th 2025

England's oldest outdoor market in shambles. Lunch time vendors and patrons alike whipped into frenzy after a Badger was reported near Deb's Tea Stall. Some eyewitnesses report seeing a dog festooned in imitation badger skin only, but tis no matter, as the destruction is complete. Councilwoman Laurie Rigg stated, "In all my years, I've never seen such chaos. Tables and chairs, arms and legs, fathers and sons, all in a right cacophony of motion. Nowhere to escape as the alley's between stalls filled with panicking customers and brick-a-brack. Bedlam, I say, complete and total." Indeed, officials have announced as of twelve fifty-three, ten dead and over fifty in critical condition.

Jenny returned from work to a dark house. She kicked her shoes off one by one in the entry way. Dropped her strangely unused cudgel in its holster. Her first day as an Executive Administrative Trainee had been a trial by fire. By fourteen o'clock she'd turned off news alerts on her mobile. The constant reports of mass casualty events threatened the capabilities of 5G networks as up/down speeds stagnated with overflow: messages, alerts, and general

traffic. By the end of the day, her scout teams had no pelts to show for their efforts. This fact led Jenny to believe that the numerous badger sightings must have been a result of some shared delusional disorder. It wasn't like her officers to go to an attack site and not at least bring back evidence of the culprit. But no badger had been found.

Jenny hadn't been this exhausted in years—at once, marching upstairs and running a hot bath. She needed to relax in the worst way. She dropped in a lavender scented bath bomb. Her hand twisted off the faucet before disrobing and climbing in. Warmth rippled goosebumps up and down her naked body as she lay down—covering her eyes with a folded rag. Finally, she thought, I can tell this awful day to "Fuck right off!"

Jenny's breath kept time with the dripping faucet. But another sound soon joined the ambience of the bathroom. Jenny sighed, "Oh god he's watching that stupid show again."

The dulcet tones of Mr. Attenborough drifted up the stairs from the TV room.

They'd been on since she arrived, but her thought torrent hadn't stilled enough till now. The unmistakable brogue mumbled: *"A colorful variety of animals live in our forest. Some are familiar to us. And the most dangerous of these four-legged fiends, remains Meles meles, or, the common European badger."*

Even here in the safety of a relaxing bath, Jenny could not be shed of her day job.

"William!" She called aloud. "Turn that rot off now I don't have the bandwidth tonight to hear any more about stupid stinking badgers!"

The TV went on without ceasing: *"To describe this stout and stocky little creature, with a smallish head and eyes blacker than a doll's eyes, as territorial excuses the pure havoc they wreak…"*

Now Jenny was no longer just knackered she was plenty miffed as well.

"William!" She shouted this time. Her tinny female voice echoed across the tiled walls. And yet no BBC relief came.

Jenny gritted her teeth. This was most out of the ordinary. William always came when she called. He knew better than to ignore her. "Elizabeth!" Jenny hollered for her daughter. Then did the same for her son, "Jenson!" Still nothing but: *"Twenty years after the 'Slaughter at Thetford Forest' and a home office declaration of emergency, no right-thinking citizen could have imagined the furry menace's killing spree continuing for this long."*

"If I have to get out of this bath to turn off the telly…" Impotent rage built inside her. "Then…then I'll fucking pull the roof down on you all!"

The words clapped back unironically. No matter— Jenny Webly didn't hear them. Lost in the splash. Too busy pulling herself upright. Water sloshed out of the tub and dripped off her middle-aged body. First one foot, then the next stood her over the now soaking bathmat. Quick as a cudgel swing her left arm collected her pink bathrobe. Hands knotted the terrycloth belt. The opening door banged and clattered behind her as she paused on the top stair.

"Can you not hear me?!"

Shadows from the TV room danced across the carpet and walls. Banister patterns strobed across family photos of smiling people ignoring her question. Except for BBC Two, the place sounded quieter than your great-grandmother's grave.

Down the hallway, her children's bedrooms remained as dark as the rest of the place. Could she be home all alone? Her first instinct remained to call Leonard. Then she remembered. Her heart squeezed a beat in her chest. "Put him out of mind," she told herself and stepped down the staircase.

The carpet felt rough against her bare feet. She'd have it all replaced once a few executive pay cheques cleared her account. She aimed to remake this modest cottage into the home she'd always wanted. A nice relaxing space for herself and children to spend their time. It went without saying her husband's role in these fantasies was minimal at best. She pictured William's sad gob staring out from the garden doghouse. Jenny kept no intentions of letting him go. Why fight and claw your feet into the PRADA high-heels if you were just going to throw out your footstool.

Jenny rounded the corner. Robe swayed as she approached the TV. In an instant, she was all alone. Or so she thought.

Familiar chittering disrupted the new quiet.

Her highly skilled head snapped in its direction.

Fingers swept damp hair behind both ears. She paused. Breath held to get a better read on the noise.

It ceased.

Had it been there at all, she wondered. Maybe the job was getting to her. She exhaled slowly. Streetlight bled in through the big window. She pulled her robe close to her throat with one hand and the other went to close the curtain.

Just as she gripped fabric you let your presence be known. The bitch screams when you flash your teeth. You chitter as the Queen of the Cudgel falls backwards over the sofa and disappears. Instinct carries you forward. One paw, two paw, three paw, four...you stay low to the ground. Soon you push through the broken window. Nose cautiously reading the room. Her human stink everywhere you turn. Bloodthirst in your heart.

Then you hear scuttled noises drifting down from upstairs. You move for it—ready to feast.

Agony rushed up Jenny's knee and throbbed. Pain like she'd never felt before refused to be ignored. Her feeble attempt to stand kept her on the carpet. A broken leg, she thought, the only thing it could be. She didn't have time for this, not when one of those evil things darkened her towers. Her cudgel, she thought, she needed it now more than ever. Its holster lay where she'd abandoned it by her shoes.

Chittering noise grew in volume.

Hands pushed against the floor, pulling with all her might. One foot—two—pain sizzled, dropping her back to ground. Her right leg, beyond fucked, made her a tripod crawling for the back door. Behind her, glass broke. The chittering, louder than ever. Something heavy padded across the carpet and stopped.

Jenny froze. Breath held. Heartbeat raced.

Upstairs bathroom—the only light. Eyes barely adjusted to the dim. Shapes made out but not much else. Jenny glanced about for something—anything. Then she saw it. One of her children's toys—a small wooden badger—of course she knew it would be this. After a lifetime spent culling the dreaded beast, a harmless one was now her only hope of escape. Fingers reached for purchase. Receipt made. End over end it sailed through the darkness. A soft blur as it hit the staircase bouncing off the wall and clattering unseen in the dark house.

The beast moved. Another blur scurrying up the staircase—chitter, chitter, chitter.

At once, Jenny made her move. Pain screamed into her thigh and pelvis. Both arms clawing across cold tile. The kitchen floor offered no grip. The thing upstairs could only be fooled for so long. She knew this. At this exact moment, it's all she knew. She didn't notice her fingernails breaking as she pulled herself forward. Wet hair veiled her face as she finally neared her target. Her trusty cudgel—the one notched tip to tip with dead badgers—whispered between her ears: *There was always room for one more Jenny.*

Behind her, a sinister shadow barreled back down the staircase.

Bloody fingers gripped her weapon as she rolled over to face it. A deep streak of Jenny's blood separated them now. Eyes met. Yellow fangs bared. She needed a better vantage point. But it was what it was.

She'd only get one chance.

The demon rushed forward—claws click-clacking across bloodied tile.

Time slowed. Teeth gritted. Cudgel swung.

Keeeerack! Fireworks popped. Blood sprayed in all directions.

And then it was over.

Jenny Welby was no longer there.

The little blonde girl who'd married into a life of disappointment was gone.

Now the lump of flesh on the kitchen floor, covered in blood like birthing fluid, had been reborn the baddest bitch on this planet. Badger brains oozed down the cudgel's handle. If only Leonard was still alive to see the dead beast twitching at her feet.

Jenny crowed in triumph,

"Fuck right off!"

J.D. Graves is an award winning filmmaker, and indie author of MAYHEM SAM a splatter western novel published by Death's Head Press. His play TALL PINES LODGE was an official selection of the New York International Fringe Festival and FronteraFEST respectively. Films produced have programmed across the US with CAPTIVE MARKET recently having its West Coast premiere as an official selection of the Newport Beach Film Festival. J.D. continues to write and live in the woods of East Texas with his wife and family.

They all say they feel normal for a while...

Dispensary of Death
adapted by E.F. Sweetman
from a script by Simon O'Neill

Sweny's Dispensary was deadly dull for a Friday. Dust motes floated peacefully in the morning sunlight, and the only sound was somber ticking of the antique wall clock.

Mr. Cartmel, the dispensary's manager, was in his office working on the invoices as Mrs. Fleming, a daily customer, poked among the toiletries, balms and salves, which really meant she was opening and sampling the products.

Laura, the pretty young pharmacist, stood at the treatment counter. She hadn't bothered with make up that morning. Her hair was pushed up in a messy bun, and she wore the dispensary's big, frumpy lab coat because her own was at the bottom of her laundry basket. Instead of reminding Mrs. Fleming to leave the merchandise alone, she chewed on the end of her pen and examined her chipped nail polish and ragged cuticles while she watched the screen on her silent mobile.

She sighed. Two weeks of fun texts with a fellow she believed would be her perfect match. He was a banker! His hobbies were Nordic mythology and maintaining his pandemic sour dough starter. Absolutely no photos or mentions of Manchester United with his mates on any of his socials. Laura made sure of that before she sent sexy boudoirs. Tonight was supposed to be their first meet-in-real-life: Dinner at

McGann's, drinks at her place afterwards, then... she could only imagine because he completely ghosted her two days ago. The Good Morning Beautiful! and Sweet Dreams, my sweet! texts along with all his funny, endearing messages throughout the day stopped without warning. She tried to call him last night (after a bottle of courage wine), and went straight to voicemail. So that was that. Probably married and got caught.

Mrs. Fleming cast a furtive glance around the dispensary before she unscrewed a new brand of acne ointment, took a loud sniff, and rubbed a dab on her chin. Laura saw it all, but she was too miserable to make an effort to scold the older woman for opening the vendibles.

The dreary silence (save the ticking of the clock and Mrs. Fleming's sniffing products) was shattered as the front door banged open, and a tall young man sporting a magnificent halo of fluffy copper hair shoved Mrs. Fleming aside as he lunged toward the treatment counter.

"Really!" squawked Mrs. Fleming. "Laura, I was here first, and he just pushed me aside like some kind of brute."

But Laura was not interested in Mrs. Fleming's complaint as she appraised the newcomer and his spectacular head of hair; a good seven inches of luxurious fluff backlit by the golden sunlight that streamed through the dispensary's front window.

"Mrs. Fleming, I'm with a customer now, you're just going to have to wait," she said as she greeted the stranger with a warm, welcoming smile.

The man opened his mouth to explain, but Mrs. Fleming cut in, "Well, isn't that just the limit? You young people! Always rushing and shoving about these days, with no con-sid-er-aaaaa-tion..."

"Mrs. Fleming! I am attending to this customer, then I will be with you directly. Only got one pair of hands here." Laura held up her hands to demonstrate that she was not hiding any more hands beneath the counter, then leaned toward her new arrival with, "Now then, what can I do you for?"

"Well, the nerve..." The offended Mrs. Fleming bustled

to cosmetics to try on the lipsticks.

"Now then..." Laura noticed that beneath that gorgeous hair, the man's face was sweaty and a sickly shade of gray. He panted heavily, as if he ran all the in way from Clontarf.

Reassured by her tenderness, he stepped closer. "Well, let's see, where do I start? Could be nothing, nothing at all! But, you read about this stuff these days, with all those stories on the news..."

Laura wasn't sure what news he was talking about because *The Irish Times* had been out of print for a month. Its online edition was just ads for bathroom caulk and Ballymaloe Original Relish, and there hadn't been a proper broadcast from RTÉ News for weeks. But she didn't want to divert him from revealing his troubles. "Oh well, we're not judgemental here, and I always find if I'm in a bit of a pickle, I feel better if I just get it off my chest."

His worried gaze moved down where she pinned her Hi! I'm Laura! badge over her left breast. He smiled despite whatever ailed him. "Well

then...Laura..."

She nodded supportively until he slapped his right hand on the counter, as if presenting her with a freshly caught trout. Mrs. Fleming heard the thwack! and scampered back to the counter.

Laura lost all pro-fessional decorum at the sight of a large, putrescent wound on the back of his hand. "Oh my...that's... nasty."

The poor fellow nodded in despair.

She shuddered as she stared at it. "Fresh?"

Mrs. Fleming popped her head over his shoulder to ogle the deep, oozing red and yellow gouge surrounded by blackened, festering blisters. It gave off the faint, foul odor of a dead mouse.

"Jack Russell?" Laura asked, "Scrappy little fun bags, aren't they? Great characters, though," she added because Jack Russell Terrier owners tended to be as mean and easily offended as their dogs.

He shook his magnificent curls. "No, it wasn't an animal, by definition. It was one of those... things."

"Things? What things?"

"The creatures, those

strange, shuffling, trance-like beings..."

Well, wasn't that just a perfect description of her last boyfriend (Jeremy? Jason? It began with a J, anyway)? Always lurching into parked cars because he never pulled his face off his mobile. Didn't even notice her leave their last dinner together because he was too engrossed with snarling at the football match while gnawing a leg of lamb. Laura shook her head to refocus on this new fellow's predicament instead of her pathetic love life.

"... and seems to be more and more of them every day, and this morning, as I was putting out my recycling, I was accosted."

Spectacular hair with brains underneath. Laura was duly impressed. "*Accosted.*"

"Exactly. I fought it off, but another one showed up, couldn't have been more than ten years old. Just a little girl, really, came out of nowhere, and anyway, she bit me."

"I see..." Laura examined the deep, revolting ulceration that appeared to spread up his arm as he revealed the details of the assault.

"Took quite a mouthful," he said as if that wasn't obvious, "and they say you only have a certain amount of time before...you know... You turn into one of them."

"According to the news," she said.

He nodded.

"Yes, well we've had a few cases in recently," she said. "I wonder what are they? And where are they coming from? American tourists maybe?"

"Oh, it's much more than a few obnoxious out-of-towners," he said. "We've been destabilizing the delicate balance between nature and over development for decades now, it was only a matter of time before the planet fought back with a horrible vengeance."

"Oh dear." Laura flinched, but couldn't help herself. "Vegan?"

He nodded and opened his jacket to show off his tie-dyed Powered By Plants T-shirt. Mrs. Fleming rolled her eyes and returned to root through the medical supplies.

"Ah, I see." Laura's hopes deflated. "So, you're into that sort of thing, are you?"

He blinked at her, apparently not comprehending.

"The planet? Gerry Torn berg, and all that?"

"It's Greta Tunberg," he corrected. "And yes, of course. Well, I'm not a fanatic or anything, but it does seem obvious to me that if we don't start doing something about this..."

Laura gazed at the ceiling, affirming her oath to never endure another kale and beet salad in search of love, or a fabulous head of hair.

"Everything all right out there, Laura?" Mr. Cartmel called out as he rolled in his swivel chair from the office to the clinic area.

"Yes, Mr. Cartmel. It's another one that's been bitten by one of those things."

"Oh dear..." Mr. Cartmel craned his neck to examine the man's wound. "Ah-ha. Well, yes then, you know what to do."

"Me, Mr. Cartmel?"

"Yes, you, Laura. Those invoices don't sort themselves, do they?"

Always an excuse when it came to actual labor, Laura thought, but said, "In the head then, Mr. Cartmel?

"Yes, that seems to do the trick if you wouldn't mind,"

Mr. Cartmel said. He lingered instead of rolling back to his invoices, apparently not too busy to watch her do the wet work. Mrs. Fleming stopped opening packaged hernia pessaries to see what was going on.

Laura sighed, "Yes Mr. Cartmel."

"In the head?" The man said faintly as his greasy, pallid complexion turned markedly greasier and more pallid.

"I guess..." Laura shrugged and pulled the Dispensary's Mossberg 12-gauge shotgun from under the counter. She chambered a round and took careful aim just below his hairline.

"Wait!" He held up his hands, "I mean, NO!"

Laura raised her eyes, but didn't lower the shotgun.

"I feel fine!" He attempted a carefree smile that was anything but carefree. "Come to think about it, I've never been better!" He began to hyperventilate. "In fact, I'm fit as a fiddle!"

"Look, you might feel fine now. They all say they feel normal for a while." Laura realigned her sight. "But the next thing you know, they're drooling all over me,"

"What is this then," he implored, "judge, jury and executioner?"

She squinted down the barrel, took a slow breath and said, "Life's unfair."

"But it's so nihilistic, so fatalistic."

Laura pondered as she lowered the gun. "It is pretty fatal, all right... and I often wonder about it myself, like where do we go? Is there really an afterlife, and if so, where do we go?"

Both Mrs. Fleming and Mr. Cartmel, bored at their existential conversation instead of a shotgun blast to his head, returned to their respective affairs of poking through merchandise and shuffling through invoices.

"No, Laura," he said, ready to delve deeply into existential philosophy instead of a receiving a face full of shot gun pellets. "What I mean is, you don't have to do this. Not if there's another way. Nothing is written, right?"

"Well, actually, I know a lot that's written, like umm..."

"Books!" Mrs. Fleming called out as if she were a quiz show contestant, the feather in her trilby bounced merrily as she scampered back to the counter. "Newspapers. Magazines."

"Exactly," Laura said. "Books, magazines, newspapers, need I go on?"

He looked desperate. "No, no. What I meant is nothing is predestined, pre-ordained as it were. We are sentient human beings. We can control our own destiny..."

"Oh for God's sake, Laura," Mrs. Fleming said, "will you just do him in so the rest of us can get on with our business?"

"Mrs. Fleming, I am with a customer right now, and will do my own diagnostics and treatment! Now, if you would stop interrupting, I can deal with..." Laura raised the shot gun again.

"It's Kevin," he said.

"I'm sorry?"

"I'm Kevin. My name is Kevin. Don't wear it out! Or do wear it out," he begged her. "Right down to the last consonant if you like." And he squeaked out one more, "*Kevin*!"

"Let me deal with Kevin first so I can see you more promptly."

"If this isn't the very limit..."

Mrs. Fleming fumed.

Laura leaned over and whispered to Kevin, "Her husband passed away just last year, poor thing, but my God, she does do my head in. She's here before me every morning, moaning all the time."

"He's only trying to humanize himself, you know, our Kevin," Mrs. Fleming said over the whispers.

Laura spoke up,"What's that you're saying now, Mrs. Fleming?"

"I said he's only trying to make you feel more empathy for him by telling you his name so you won't do him in like the others. Oldest trick in the book."

"Yes! Thank you for your input Mrs. Fleming." Laura whispered back to Kevin, "See what I mean? Nosey old bag."

"I heard that!" Mrs. Fleming screeched, her teeth smudged with the latest shade of Coral Passion lipstick.

"The others?" Kevin wheezed.

Laura took aim again. "Look babe, I'm sorry."

"No!" Kevin shrieked. "Isn't there something you can do to cure it? To cure me? Isn't that what you would want too?"

She studied Kevin thoughtfully. "Well, yes... there is an experimental treatment I found in my research..." She called out to the office, "What do you think, Mr. Cartmel, should we try the emergency apositia?"

Mr. Cartmel rolled back into the clinic. "What's this now, Laura?" He cleaned his glasses as he considered her idea. "Another wounded bird with a broken wing for your menagerie? Well, I suppose you could try it again. Just make sure you go well above the contagion site this time."

"Yes, Mr. Cartmel."

"You're too bloody sensitive, that's your problem."

Laura shrugged and smiled bashfully.

"She cares too much. It's not a job for her, it's a vocation," Mr. Cartmel said to Kevin.

Kevin gazed at her. "Oh yes, indeed, I can see that."

"Now, I can't guarantee anything," she warned.

"Of course," Kevin said. "You're just doing your best in these trying circumstances."

Mrs. Fleming groaned. "I could be home now... With my feet up, watching Bargain Hunt."

Mr. Cartmel, Laura, and Kevin exchanged glances because Bargain Hunt hadn't been broadcasted for months. Then Laura said to Kevin, "I just don't want you to think I'm cutting any corners."

"Thank you Laura," Kevin said. "I somehow knew that, when I first saw you, when I first came in. You gave out an aura. Laura's aura, you could call it..."

"Christ. Poetry. That's a new one," muttered Mrs. Fleming.

"I could see the compassion in your eyes," Kevin went on, "because the eyes never lie, they're the windows to the soul."

"Ooooh, windows to the soul. Isn't that nice, Mrs. Fleming?" Laura cooed.

Mrs. Fleming muttered, "Pass me the sick bucket."

"See what I mean?" Laura said to Kevin. "She's gone awful cynical, poor love, ever since her Tommy cashed in his chips."

Kevin nodded, desperate for any option other than getting his head blasted off.

"Anyway..." Laura set the shotgun aside and slammed a big cutting board on the counter. "Prop it on that, like a good lad."

Mr. Cartmel replaced his glasses and Mrs. Fleming leaned in with wide eyes and a big grin as Kevin flopped his rotting hand onto the board.

Laura pulled out a massive meat cleaver. "Now, you're only going to feel a little sting," she reassured as she swung the cleaver up so fast it whistled. Then the heavy blade chopped into his right forearm with a loud, meaty CRACK.

Kevin watched in horror as Laura chopped, snapping bones and popping through tendons. His blood spewed all over her hands, face, and the front of her lab coat. His screams shook the front window glass. "Jesus, God!" he howled, and resumed screaming as Laura excised his afflicted appendage.

"Well, there's no need for that kind of language," Mrs. Fleming declared, offended..

Finally, they all watched his hand bounce off the cutting board, land on the floor with fingers grasping upwards as if attempting to crawl back where it belonged on Kevin's arm.

"All done," Laura said

cheerfully as she stomped the foot pedal of the metal hazardous waste bin to open the lid. She seized Kevin's hand with the dispensary's reacher/grabber tool and dropped it in with a loud, surprisingly heavy thud, "That wasn't so bad, was it?"

"Aaaaaaaahhhhhh! Wasn't so bad? *Wasn't so bad?*" Kevin babbled senselessly, "Aaaaaaaaaahhhhh!"

Laura was taken aback, "Well, I wouldn't have bothered if I'd known you'd make such a fuss."

He gaped at the gory dog-end of his arm. "Christ's armchair!" He shook the bloody stump at her, "Well how am I supposed to react, huh?"

"Maybe with a little more gratitude," she said icily.

"You cut my fucking hand off! You-you mutilated me!"

"...And a lot less drama, I should say, considering the alternative," she added as she patted the Mossberg.

His eyes crossed as he blithered, "Kehhrrrrns-lidder-aaahhh thaa aaahhh..."

"Now, let's get a bandage on that, shall we?"

"...Napoleon's balls, I fink

I'm a goncrrrr..." Kevin's eyes rolled back and he dropped to the floor.

After the excitement, Mr. Cartmel scooted into his office while Mrs. Fleming patiently awaited for her turn in line. She observed to Laura that her Tommy looked better dead than Kevin looked unconscious.

After a few minutes, Kevin stirred. "Oh, I'm sorry. I seemed to have, ahhh, I guess fainted there..." He looked at his bandaged stump, and yelled "Christ's armchair!"

Mrs. Fleming said, "Your boyfriend is awake, Laura."

Kevin gazed up from the floor. "Laura... you know something? You're beautiful."

Laura removed her blood-spattered glasses, and batted her eyes. "Oh my, aren't you a charmer?"

"That was a little extreme, but you took control of the situation, and look at me now, I'm better already."

Laura nodded and smiled at him.

He jumped to his feet. "People do say you should use the your pharmacist for this type of thing instead of clogging up the GP surgeries."

"Well, we are health care professionals," she modestly acknowledged.

"Absolutely. And I realize now that you did what you had to do to protect me."

Laura nodded sympathetically. "It hurt me more than it hurt you, Kevin."

As he mentally relived the amputation, without even a smear of numbing cream, he said, "I very much doubt that…but you did it to staunch the infection, before the poison could take over."

"Exactly," Laura said, then added a self-deprecating, "Duh…"

They smiled at one another in mutual a discovery that they were very much in harmony, and maybe a little in love.

Mrs. Fleming destroyed the moment with, "Well, I for one don't know what all this fuss is for. Yes, the whole world's gone mad, and now my little grandkids have turned into those things, but what of it? I mean, yes, I do have to keep them locked in the coal shed, but that's for their own good." Mrs. Fleming chuckled as she went on, "Why that little

Darren took quite a nip out of me this morning, but here I am, alive and well, right as rain. I just washed it with the TCP antiseptic you sold me."

Laura shook her head, "When was that exactly?"

"Then I put a little Savlon on it, and that was that."

Laura shook her head again, "When did you buy TCP and Savlon, Mrs. Fleming?"

Mrs. Fleming was not to be deterred by insignificant questions. "Of course, things were quite different in my day. We didn't run to see a therapist every time Daddy didn't buy us a pony. No, no, we were too busy bringing up our families."

Kevin's face began to turn pale and clammy, but he continued bravely: "I'm going to survive this. It's all because of you Laura, because you're kind, beautiful, and caring."

"Oh Kevin, I'm only doing my job."

"And from this day forth…" Kevin held up his right stump, looked at it, then held up his left index finger. "From this day forward, I am changing the way I think about the world, about humanity, about my fellow man." He smiled at

Laura. "*And* woman."

With that declaration, both Laura and Mrs. Fleming could not help but smile at him.

"Laura..." Kevin took a deep breath as if to make an announcement. "I...aaaargh," he clenched his stomach and released a long, loud fart.

"A couple of Rennies should take care of that," Mrs. Fleming advised.

"I'll be the one to determine what Kevin needs, Mrs. Fleming," Laura reminded her.

Kevin tried again, "I think...gaahh...that is...err-aaagghh..."

"I'm sorry Kevin, I'm not following you," Laura said.

"Whew! I seem to have lost my ability to form a sentence." Kevin took a deep breath. Began, a third time, but his tongue looked dark, and too big for his mouth. "Lawrah, whah I'm dwrying to thay ith I woo very mush like to thee you again." Then he farted long and loud.

Laura's experience with emergency apositia was limited, but she knew it could induce a myriad of autonomic bodily functions in response to the trauma, so she smiled and encouraged Kevin to go on, as it was part of the healing process.

"I don't fink I ever met a woman who tho lovingly combinesth compathion..."

"Oh, Kevin," she said.

"Beauty."

"Well, you're embarrassing me now."

"And..." He licked spittle running down his chin and whispered, "bwains."

"Yes, well I do have my Masters from PSI."

Kevin garbled then belched, "ggbb www-aaains!"

"All right," Laura said, reaching under the counter for the bottle of Rennies antacids.

Kevin's head rolled as he made a few more guttural sounds, then he gurgled, "*gaahhhhhbwwwaaaahhhains!*"

"Better not overdo yourself," Laura warned.

Kevin folded over, then shot upright as if a hot poker went up his ass. His face was cadaverously ashen. Red-rimmed eyelids surrounded blank white, lifeless eyes. He bared his teeth in a repulsive grimace and roared, "Bwains! Bwrrains! Brrrrraaaaaaaains!"

Laura sighed and grabbed the shotgun. As she took

careful aim, she said, "Nobody can say we didn't try," and blasted his face off. "Good bye sweetie."

Kevin collapsed again. This time for good. As Laura peered at him over the counter, she felt a tiny spark of joy in the tragedy. Although she could not save Kevin, she managed to spare his beautiful hair.

Mr. Cartmel called out from his office, "That was him gone, Laura?"

"Yes, Mr. Cartmel."

"Right in the head, was it?"

"Yes, Mr. Cartmel."

"Very good. That seems to do the trick all right."

Mrs. Fleming stepped over Kevin's body to to the front of the line and presented a tiny bottle of rubbing alcohol. "Just this for now please, Laura."

"That'll be 89c, Mrs. Fleming," Laura said.

Mrs. Fleming set her bag on the counter to pull out her coin purse.

Laura dropped her face into her hands. "Well isn't that typical, I finally meet a fellow I can really relate to, and what happens? He turns into an undead, a hellish creature with a ravenous appetite for human brains. Definitely not vegan, isn't that right Mrs. Fleming?"

"Mmm hmm," Mrs. Fleming answered as she counted her change.

"My God, there's unlucky in love, and then there's Laura."

"Humph," Mrs. Fleming said as she lost count of the amount of pennies on the counter.

"I guess it's back to Tinder or Bumble."

"Shushhh!" Mrs. Fleming glared at her, recounting her coins.

"Sitting at home with a glass of wine, I always end up thinking, right! I'll just give it one more go, but this is the last time! I suppose things were different in your day, Mrs. Fleming…"

Mrs. Fleming did not answer. Laura looked up. Her bag and coin purse on the the counter, but Mrs. Fleming was nowhere in sight.

"Mrs. Fleming?"

Instead of an answer Laura heard a snarl, then a *snap*, followed by loud crunching and wet sucking slurps.

Laura peeked over the counter to see Mrs. Fleming crouched over Kevin's body like a giant spider as blood, bone fragments, and brain matter drooled from her mouth onto her scarf and coat. She split Kevin's skull like a cantaloupe and plunged her face into his spongey grey matter, thus ruining Laura's final reminder of Kevin: his magnificent hair.

Laura looked up in frustration as she grabbed the shot gun and called out, "Just seems to be one thing after the next Mr. Cartmel."

Mr. Cartmel came out of his office and beheld the sight of Mrs. Fleming cramming handfuls of Kevin's brains into her mouth. "Oh, it's always bloody murder on a Friday, Laura."

At the sound of the click! clack! of the shotgun, Mrs. Fleming lifted onto her fingers and toes. Slimy tendrils of Kevin's flesh, brains, and blood trailed down her chin and pooled onto matted tufts of hair on the floor. She snarled as Laura took aim, then leapt just as Laura blew her head to smithereens.

"Well, that's that," Mr. Cartmel said. "Back to the invoices, and it looks like you've got work to do out here as well."

"I suppose so, Mr. Cartmel," Laura said, surveying the carnage. "Always bloody murder on a Friday."

E.F. Sweetman lives in Beverly, Massachusetts. Her short stories have appeared in *Pulp Modern*, FunDead Publications, *Switchblade Magazine*, *Econoclash Review*, and *Broadswords and Blasters*. She's been a fishmonger, a picture framer, and a nurse until she took the leap into writing crime and noir full time. She is currently at work on a hardboiled crime trilogy.

*Tonight you will go forth, my sons,
and slay this fabulous werewolf...*

The Werewolf Howls
Clifford Ball

The men who were waiting for that wolf had silver bullets in their muskets.

Twilight had come upon the slopes of the vineyards, and a gentle, caressing breeze drifted through the open casement to stir into further disorder the papers upon the desk where Monsieur Etienne Delacroix was diligently applying himself. He raised his leonine head, the hair of which had in his later years turned to gray, and stared vacantly from beneath bushy brows at the formation of a wind-driven cloud as if he thought that the passive elements of the heavens could, if they so desired, aid him in some momentous decision.

There was a light but firm tap on the door which led to the hall of the château. Monsieur Delacroix blinked as his thoughts were dispersed and, in some haste, gathered various documents together and thrust them into the maw of a large envelope before bidding the knocker to enter.

Pierre, his eldest son, came quietly into the room. The father felt a touch of the pride he could never quite subdue when Pierre approached, for he had a great faith in his son's probity, as well as an admiration for the straight carriage and clear eye he, at his own age, could no longer achieve. Of late he had been resting a great many matters pertaining to the management of the Château Doré and the

business of its vineyards, which supported the estate, on the broad shoulders poised before him.

But Etienne Delacroix had been born in a strict household and his habits fashioned in a stern school, and was the lineal descendant of ancestors who had planted their peasant's feet, reverently but independently, deep into the soil of France; so visible emotions were to him a betrayal of weakness. There was no trace of the deep regard he felt for his son evident when he addressed the younger man.

"Where are your brothers? Did I not ask you to return with them?"

"They are here, Father. I entered first, to be certain that you were ready to receive us."

"Bid them enter."

Jacques and François came in to stand with their elder brother and were careful to remain a few inches in his rear; he was the acknowledged spokesman. Their greetings were spoken simultaneously; Jacques' voice breaking off on a high note which caused him obvious embarrassment, for he was adolescent. Together,

thought Monsieur Delacroix, they represented three important steps in his life, three payments on account to posterity. He was glad his issue had all been males; since the early death of his wife he had neither cared for any woman nor taken interest in anything feminine.

"I have here, my son, some papers of importance," he announced, addressing Pierre. "As you observe, I am placing them here where you may easily obtain them in the event of my absence." Suiting the action to the word, he removed the bulky envelope to a drawer in the desk and turned its key, allowing the tiny piece of metal to remain in its lock. "I am growing older"— his fierce, challenging eyes swept the trio as if he dared a possible contradiction—"and it is best that you are aware of these accounts, which are relative to the business of the château,"

"He flung back his head— whimpering,"

"Non, non!" chorused all three. "You are as young as ever, papa!"

"Sacre blue! Do you name me a liar, my children? Attend,

Pierre!"

"Yes, papa."

"I have work for you this night."

The elder son's forehead wrinkled. "But the work, it is over. Our tasks are completed. The workers have been checked, the last cart is in the shed——"

"This is a special task, one which requires the utmost diligence of you all. It is of the wolf."

"The werewolf!" exclaimed Jacques, crossing himself.

The other brothers remained silent, but mingled expressions of wonder and dislike passed across their features. Ever since the coming of the wolf the topic of its depredations had been an unwelcome one in the household of the Château Doré.

"Mon Dieu, Jacques!" exploded the head of the house. "Have you, too, been listening to the old wives' tales? Must you be such an imbecile, and I your father? Rubbish! There can be no werewolves; has not the most excellent Father Cromecq flouted such stones ten thousand times? It is a common wolf; a large one, true, but nevertheless

a common mongrel, a beast from the distant moun-tain. Of its ferocity we are unfortunately well aware; so it must be dispatched with the utmost alacrity."

"But, the workers say, papa, that there have been no wolves in the fields for more than a hundred——"

"Peste! The ever verbose workers! The animal is patently a vagrant, a stray beast driven from the mountains by the lash of its hunger. And I, Etienne Delacroix, have pronounced that it must die!"

The father passed a heavy hand across his forehead, for he was weary from his unaccustomed labor over the accounts. His hands trembled slightly, the result of an old nervous disorder. The fingers were thick, and blunt from the hardy toil of earlier years; the blue veins were still corded from the strength which he had once possessed.

"It is well," said Pierre in his own level tones. "Since the wolf came upon and destroyed poor little Marguerite D'Estourie, tearing her throat to shreds, and the gendarmes who almost cornered it were unable to slap it because they could not shoot straight, and it persists in——"

"It slashed the shoulder of old Gavroche who is so feeble he cannot walk without two canes!" interrupted François, excitedly.

"——ravaging our ewes," concluded the single-minded Pierre, who was not to be sidetracked once he had chosen his way, whether in speech or action. "The damage to our flocks has been great, papa. It is just that we should take action, since the police have failed. I have thought this wolf strange, too, although I place no faith in demons. If it but seeks food, why must it slay so wantonly and feed so little? It is indeed like a great, gray demon in appearance. Twice have I viewed it, leaping across the meadows in the moonlight, its long, gray legs hurling it an unbelievable distance at every bound. And Marie Polydore, of the kitchens, found its tracks only yesterday at the very gates of the château!"

"I have been told," revealed Jacques, flinging his hands about in adolescent earnestness, "that the wolf is the beast-soul of one who has been stricken by the moon-demons. By day he is as other men, but by night, though he has the qualities of a saint he cannot help himself. Perhaps he is one with whom we walk and talk, little guessing his dreadful affliction."

"Silence!" roared Monsieur Delacroix. One of his clenched fists struck the desk a powerful blow and the sons were immediately quieted. "Must I listen to the ranting and raving and driveling of fools and imbeciles? Am I not still the master of the Château Doré? I will tend to the accursed matter as I have always, will I not? I have always seen to the welfare of the dwellers in the shadow of the Château Doré! And with the help of the good God I shall continue to do so, until the last drop of my blood has dried away from my bones. You comprehend?"

In a quieter tone, after the enforced silence, he continued: "I have given orders to both the foreman and Monsieur the mayor that this night, the night of the full moon by which we may detect the marauder, all the people of the vineyards and of the town beyond must remain behind locked windows and barred doors. If they have obeyed my orders—and may the good God look after those who have not—they are even now secure in the safety of their respective homes. Let me discover but one demented idiot peeking from behind his shutter and I promise you he shall have cause to remember his disobedience!"

Pierre nodded without speaking, knowing he was being instructed to punish a possible, but improbable, offender.

"Now, we are four intelligent men, I trust," said Monsieur Delacroix, pretending not to notice the glow of pleasure which suffused Jacques' features at being included in their number. "We are the Delacroix's, which is sufficient. And as leaders we must, from time to time, grant certain concessions to the inferior mentalities of the unfortunate who dwell in ignorance; so I have this day promised the good foremen, who petitioned me regarding the activities of this wolf, to perform certain things. They firmly believe the gray wolf is a demon, an inhuman atrocity visited upon

us by the Evil One. And also, according to their ancient but childish witch-lore, that it may only be destroyed by a silver weapon."

Monsieur Delacroix reached beneath his chair and drew forth a small, but apparently heavy, sack. Upending it on the surface of the desk, he scattered in every direction a double dozen glittering cylindrical objects.

"Bullets!" exclaimed Jacques.

"Silver bullets!" amended Pierre.

"Yes, my son. Bullets of silver which I molded myself in the cellars, and which I have shown to the men, with the promise that they will be put to use."

"Expensive weapons," commented the thrifty François.

"It is the poor peasant's belief. If we slew tills wolf with mere lead or iron they would still be frightened of their own shadows and consequently worthless at their work, as they have been for the past month. Here are the guns. Tonight you will go forth, my sons, and slay this fabulous werewolf, and cast its carcass upon the cartload of dry wood I have had piled by the vineyard road, and burn it until there is nothing left but the ash, for all to see and know."

"Yes, papa,"Assented Pierre and François as one, but the boy Jacques cried: "What? So fine a skin? I would like it for the wall of my room! These who have seen the wolf say its pelt is like silver shaded into gray——"

"Jacques!" Etienne Delacroix's anger flooded his face with a great surge of red and bulging veins, and Pierre and François were stricken with awe at the sight of their father's wrath.

"If you do not burn this beast as I say, immediately after slaying it, I will forget you are my son, and almost a man! I will——"

His own temper choked him into incoherency.

"I crave your pardon, father," begged Jacques, humbled and alarmed. "I forgot myself."

"We will obey, papa, as always," said François, quickly, and Pierre gravely nodded.

"The moon will soon be up," said Monsieur Delacroix, after a short silence. The room had grown dark while they talked; receiving a wordless signal from his father, Pierre struck a match and lit the blackened lamp on the desk. With the startling transition, as light leaped forth to dispel the murky shadows of the room, Pierre came near to exclaiming aloud at sight of the haggard lines in his father's face. For the first time in his life he realized that what his parent had said earlier in the evening about aging was not spoken jocularly, not the repeated jest Monsieur Delacroix had always allowed himself, but the truth. His father was old.

"You had better go," said Etienne Delacroix, as his keen eyes caught the fleeting expression on his son's face. His fingers drummed a muffled tattoo upon the fine edge of his desk, the only sign of his nervous condition that he could not entirely control. "Monsieur the Mayor's opinion is that the wolf is stronger when the moon is full. But it is mine that tonight it will be easier to discover."

The three turned to the door, but as they reached the threshold Monsieur Delacroix beckoned to the eldest. "An instant, Pierre. I speak to you alone."

The young man closed the door on his brothers' backs and returned to the desk, his steady eyes directed at his father.

Monsieur Delacroix, for the moment, seemed to have forgotten what he intended to say. His head was bowed on his chest and the long locks of his ashen hair had fallen forward over his brow. Suddenly he sat erect, as if it took an immense effort of his will to perform the simple action, and again Pierre was startled to perceive the emotions which twisted his father's features.

It was the first time he had ever seen tenderness there, or beheld love in the eyes he had sometimes, in secret, thought a little cruel.

"Have you a pocket crucifix, my son?"

"In my room."

"Take it with you tonight. And—you will stay close to Jacques, will you not?" His voice was hoarse with unaccustomed anxiety. "He is young, confident, and— careless. I would not wish to endanger your good mother's last child."

Pierre was amazed. It had been fifteen years since he had last heard his father mention his mother.

"You have been a good son, Pierre. Obey me now. Do not let the three of you separate, for I hear this beast is a savage one and unafraid even of armed men. Take care of yourself, and see to your brothers."

"Will you remain in the château for safety, papa? You are not armed."

"I am armed by my faith in the good God and the walls of Château Doré. When you have lit the fire under the wolf's body—I will be there."

He lowered the leonine head once more, and Pierre, not without another curious look, departed.

For a long while Monsieur Delacroix sat immobile, his elbows resting on the padded arras of the chair, the palms of his hands pressing into his cheeks. Then he abruptly arose and, approaching the open casement, drew the curtains wide. Outside, the long, rolling slopes fell away toward a dim horizon already blanketed by the dragons of night, whose tiny, flickering eyes were winking into view one by one in the dark void above. Hurrying cloudlets scurried in little groups across the sky.

Lamps were being lit in the jumble of cottages that were the abodes of Monsieur Delacroix's workmen, but at the moment the sky was illuminated better than the earth; for the gathering darkness seemed to ding like an animate thing to the fields and meadows, and stretch ebony claws across the ribbon of the roadway.

It was time for the moon to rise.

Monsieur Delacroix turned away from the casement and with swift, certain steps went to the door, opening it. The hall was still, but from the direction of the dining room there came a clatter of dishes as the servants cleared the table. Quickly, with an unusual alacrity for a man of his years, he silently traversed the floor of the huge hall and passed through its outer portals. A narrow gravel lane led him along the side of the château until he reached the building's extreme corner, where he abandoned it to strike off across the closely clipped sward in the direction of a small clump of beech trees.

The night was warm and peaceful, with no threat of rain. A teasing zephyr tugged at the thick locks on his uncovered head; from somewhere near his feet came the chirp of a cricket.

In the grove it was darker until he came to its center, wending through and past the entangled thickets like one who had traveled the same path many times, and found the small glade that opened beneath the stars. Here there was more light again but no breeze at all. In the center of the glade was an oblong, grassy mound, and at one end of it a white stone, and on the stone the name of his wife.

Monsieur Delacroix stood for an instant beside the grave with lowered head, and then he sank to his knees and began to pray.

In the east the sky began to brighten as though some torch-bearing giant drew near, walking with great strides beyond the edge of the earth. The stars struggled feebly against the superior illumination, but their strength diminished as a narrow band of encroaching yellow fire appeared on the rim of the world.

With its arrival the low monotone of prayer was checked, to continue afterward with what seemed to be some difficulty. Monsieur Delacroix's throat was choked, either with grief for the unchangeable past or an indefinable apprehension for the inevitable future. His breath came in struggling gasps and tiny beads of perspiration formed on his face and hands. His prayers became mumbled, jerky utterances, holding no recognizable phrases of speech. Whispers, and they ceased altogether.

A small dark cloud danced across a far-off mountain-top, slid furtively over the border of the land, and for a minute erased the yellow gleam from the horizon. Then, as if in terror, shaken by its own temerity, it fled frantically into oblivion, and the great golden platter of the full moon issued from behind the darkness it had left to deluge the landscape with a ceaseless shower of illusive atoms;

tiny motes that danced the pathways of space.

Monsieur Delacroix gave a low cry like a child in pain. His agonized eyes were fixed on the backs of his two hands as he held them pressed against the dew-dampened sward. His fingers had begun to stiffen and curl at their tips; he could see the long, coarse hairs sprouting from the pores of his flesh — as he had many times within the past month since the night he had fallen asleep by the grave of his wife and slept throughout the night under the baleful beams of the moon.

He flung back his head, whimpering because of the terrible pressure he could feel upon his skull, and its shape appeared to alter so that it seemed curiously elongated. His eyes were bloodshot, and as they sank into their sockets his lips began to twitch over the fangs in his mouth.

The three brothers, crouching nervously in the shadows of the vineyards, started violently.

Jacques, the younger, almost lost his grasp on the gun with the silver bullets which his father had given him.

From somewhere nearby there had arisen a great volume of sound, swirling and twisting and climbing to shatter itself into a hundred echoes against the vault of the heavens, rushing and dipping and sinking into the cores of all living hearts and the very souls of men—the hunting-cry of the werewolf.

Clifford Ball, inspired by Robert E. Howard, wrote Weird fiction for *Weird Tales* in the late 1930s and early 1940s, notably following Howard's unfortunate passing. Ball's work appeared exclusively in *Weird Tales*. "The Werewolf Howls" was his final published work, appearing in 1941.

MANY BOOKS CLAIM TO BE
GRINDHOUSE

THIS ONE DELIVERS

UNCLE B.
PUBLICATIONS

WHEREVER GOOD BOOKS ARE SOLD

Much of the charm of this film is derived from the interactions between Lou Costello and the Universal baddies.

Destroy All Monsters:
Abbot and Costello Meet Frankenstein

Anthony Perconti

I first encountered the comedic pair of Bud Abbot and Lou Costello at some point, back in the early to mid-1980's, if memory serves. Growing up in Northern New Jersey as the child of immigrants, my parents didn't spend their hard-earned bucks on such frivolities as cable television. They had bigger fish to fry, economically speaking. Nope, I grew up on the three major network's channels (CBS, NBC and ABC for those of you too young to remember such a thing as analog TV), the blessing that is PBS and a passel of local channels. And I'm not even going to go into the arcane glory of the UHF bandwidth spectrum (think tinny ass AM radio, but for your television). What a fantastic way to chase our Thanksgiving dinner, then by binging on Mighty Joe Young, King Kong, Son of Kong and King Kong vs. Godzilla on WOR (channel 9). Or if it was a slow and rainy Saturday afternoon? Boom! The Drive-In Movie on WNEW, channel 5 had you covered. Drive-In was all kung-fu, all of the time! This is where I (and I suspect, the members of the Wu-Tang Clan) first watched such classics as The 36th Chamber of Shaolin (aka Master Killer), Master of the Flying Guillotine and Five Deadly Venoms.

UNIVERSAL-INTERNATIONAL presents

BUD   LOU
ABBOTT and COSTELLO
meet
FRANKENSTEIN

The Wolfman   Dracula   The Monster
LON CHANEY • BELA LUGOSI • GLENN STRANGE

Directed by CHAS. T. BARTON • Produced by ROBERT ARTHUR

Just before the Drive-In time slot, WNEW would rotate in films from the Hammer and the Amicus libraries, along with Roger Corman features. WPIX, channel 11 featured Abbott and Costello movies on Sunday mornings. This is where I watched Abbott and Costello Meet Frankenstein. And boy, let me tell you, it was love at first sight.

Being a hopeless comic nerd, Abbott and Costello Meet Frankenstein scratched a particular itch for me. As a kid, there was nothing better than when Spidey joined forces with the Thing or say, Daredevil to put the beatdown on the villain of the month. Or when the (Barry Allen) Flash crossed dimensions to meet his older counterpart on a parallel Earth. These meetings were ways that stated in no uncertain terms, that company owned intellectual properties could interact with other said properties to form a sense of cohesiveness. A company wide web of interconnectedness. Team ups, were something to look forward to; they signaled something outside the normal monthly rigmarole. Hey

listen, if Supes from Earth 1 and Earth 2 had to collaborate on taking down a particular cosmic threat? You just knew that shit just got serious.

It is with this sense of comic book wonder (that stems from me being a kid) that I absorbed this crossover classic. And to be absolutely honest, after a recent re-watch, some of that old magic has worn off (but more on this in a little bit). Abbott and Costello Meet Frankenstein is a classic "monster rally" in the truest sense of the term. Dig it; a movie featuring not one, but three of the classic Universal heavy hitters. Glenn Strange stars as the green skinned and bolt necked, "Monster." More is the pity that Boris Karloff turned down the opportunity to reprise the role that put him on the map, but an absolutely understandable decision, in my view. I suspect that Karloff didn't want to tarnish his relationship with the character that made him a star. The Monster played just for laughs and a hefty paycheck? Karloff didn't go for it. Lon Chaney Jr. did come back to play the guilt ridden, hangdog Lawrence

Talbot, aka The Wolf Man. While rounding out this unholy trio, is none other than Big Bad Bela Lugosi, who returned as Count Dracula aka "Doctor Lejos." Other supporting cast members include Jane Randolph as Joan Raymond, the Lois Lane-like insurance investigator, Charles Bradstreet as the heartthrob, Dr. Stevens and Lenore Aubert as Sandra Mornay, the vivisectionist baddie. And riding herd on this motley crew is the eternal straight-man Bud Abbott as Chick Young and the goofball Lou Costello, as Wilbur Grey.

The plot (such as it is) of A and C Meet Frankenstein, revolves around Dracula's remains being shipped over to Florida to be placed on display at a local cabinet of curiosities. Things go pear-shaped post haste, when the comedic duo of Abbott and Costello, working as baggage claims attendants get involved. There is no need in doing a deep plot dive with this one; this isn't Kurosawa, Herzog or Kubrick that we're dealing with. Suffice it to say that Drac, with the aid of Doctor Mornay plan on installing Costello's brain into the Monster's cranium (for the purpose of easy compliance and mailability). Much of the action takes place on a gothic isle, a veritable "House of Dracula," off the Florida coast. Yeah, you read that right. Absolutely not a typo. Much of the charm of this film is derived from the interactions between Lou Costello and the Universal baddies. There is a great scene early on in the film, when Lugosi and Costello play a version of coffin hide and seek / boy who cried wolf. Not to mention Costello's hapless (see the term, 'sucker' or 'chump' in the dictionary) interactions with Jane Randolph and Lenore Aubert's characters. These two women know exactly what they want and know exactly how to go about getting it. There are some great set pieces in the extended island denouement sequence; the mad scientist laboratory is brimming with Jacob's Ladders and Tesla Coils spitting and shooting sparks all over the place. And the Lugosi (animated) transformation from human to bat is exceptional. And truth to tell, the scene in which

Doctor Mornay gets her just desserts by the Monster left me flabbergasted for a bit. But fear not, true believers. Our two hapless heroes turn out okay in the end. The Universal trio get their proverbial hash settled and all's well that ends well. The film's creative team even snuck in an Invisible Man cameo (voiced by the singular, Vincent Price) just as the end credits roll. And yes, in case you were wondering, Abbott and Costello did meet up with the Invisible Man in 1951, along with the Mummy in 1955. Producers just had to go back to the well. It wouldn't make financial sense not to. Let's face it, much like in the world of comics, these crossover events translate to cold hard cash for the IP owners. Abbott and Costello Meet Frankenstein is fun stuff for the whole family.

But as I alluded to earlier in the essay, some of the magic has worn off upon my re-viewing of Abbott and Costello Meet Frankenstein. It's touched by a sense of melancholy. Don't get me wrong; this is a fun feature that sure as hell doesn't take itself at all seriously. It's a silly, good spirited way to kill an hour and a half on a Friday night, no question. I had a hoot on my second go around. But one scene in particular tipped the scales for me. A scene that got stuck in my damn

craw. Dracula is being chased throughout several rooms of his castle by the Wolf-Man. Just before they take their tussle out onto the balcony (overlooking jagged rocks and crashing waves, natch), we see Lugosi chucking a flower vase at the feral Chaney. Digest that fact for a moment.

This is the same actor who practically co-invented a film subgenre in Browning's 1931 masterpiece (no disrespect to Lon Chaney Senior's The Phantom of the Opera, but when folks hear the words 'Universal Monsters,' I'd be willing to bet Lugosi, Karloff and perhaps Lanchester come directly to mind). The same man whose magnetic persona was practically a force of freaking nature. The same man whose ego compelled him until the end of his days to flaunt in his study, a nude portrait of Clara Bow as a memento of their brief affair. The Dracula from '31 would have taken the sad Wolf-Talbot apart like a watch.

Sure, Lugosi was seventeen years older in Meet Frankenstein and sure, old Bela knew this was an easy money job; a clean-cut take-the-money and run gig. Maybe it's due to the fact that watching this feature as an adult, I know that Lugosi's career never bounced back to its former glory. There were no more The Black Cat's, nor even White Zombie's in his future. That this film is his last (semi golden age) hurrah. By 1956, a mere eight years after starring in Abbott and Costello Meet Frankenstein, Lugosi succumbed to a heart attack. That hokey vase throwing scene seems almost prophetic; this was the beginning of that slow and steady downward spiral. Abbott and Costello Meet Frankenstein in my view, is neither fish, nor fowl. Although a fun as hell enjoyable watch, that certainly is in the running for best Abbott and Costello feature, it falls short on the Universal Monsters front. And sure, I get it that the monsters are meant to out straight-man, the tried-and-true Bud Abbott. A classic monster rally it may be, but just imagine if they shot a version of this film "straight," and not for laughs? But of course, that would undermine the crossover appeal and

exclude many of the folks that would have gone to see this primarily as an Abbott and Costello comedy. Imagine the three (hell, why not four? Throw the Mummy into the mix as well) Universal heavy hitters battling it out for supremacy minus the comedic interludes? Now that would be a monster rally to end all monster rallies.

All photos courtesy Universal Studios

Pulp Modern's patron saint of pulp culture, **Anthony Perconti**, lives and works in the hinterlands of New Jersey with his wife and kids. He enjoys well-crafted and engaging stories across a variety of genres and mediums. His articles have appeared in several online venues including *ThePulp. net* and *EconoClash Review*. He can be found on *X.com* at @AnthonyPerconti.

CUTTING EDGE
OUTLAW FICTION

ALL DUE
RESPECT

Crime Fiction

WWW.ADRCRIMEFICTION.COM

I cannot think of the deep sea without shuddering at the nameless things that may at this very moment be crawling and floundering on its slimy bed.

Dagon

H.P. Lovecraft

I am writing this under an appreciable mental strain, since by tonight I shall be no more. Penniless, and at the end of my supply of the drug which alone makes life endurable, I can bear the torture no longer; and shall cast myself from this garret window into the squalid street below. Do not think from my slavery to morphine that I am a weakling or a degenerate. When you have read these hastily scrawled pages you may guess, though never fully realise, why it is that I must have forgetfulness or death.

It was in one of the most open and least frequented parts of the broad Pacific that the packet of which I was supercargo fell a victim to the German sea-raider.

The great war was then at its very beginning, and the ocean forces of the Hun had not completely sunk to their later degradation; so that our vessel was made a legitimate prize, whilst we of her crew were treated with all the fairness and consideration due us as naval prisoners. So liberal, indeed, was the discipline of our captors, that five days after we were taken I managed to escape alone in a small boat with water and provisions for a good length of time.

When I finally found myself adrift and free, I had but little idea of my surroundings. Never a competent navigator, I could only guess vaguely by the sun and stars that I was somewhat south of the equator. Of the longitude

I knew nothing, and no island or coast-line was in sight. The weather kept fair, and for uncounted days I drifted aimlessly beneath the scorching sun; waiting either for some passing ship, or to be cast on the shores of some habitable land. But neither ship nor land appeared, and I began to despair in my solitude upon the heaving vastnesses of unbroken blue.

The change happened whilst I slept. Its details I shall never know; for my slumber, though troubled and dream-infested, was continuous. When at last I awaked, it was to discover myself half sucked into a slimy expanse of hellish black mire which extended about me in monotonous undulations as far as I could see, and in which my boat lay grounded some distance away.

Though one might well imagine that my first sensation would be of wonder at so prodigious and unexpected a transformation of scenery, I was in reality more horrified than astonished; for there was in the air and in the rotting soil a sinister quality which chilled me to the very core. The region was putrid with the carcasses of decaying fish, and of other less describable things which I saw protruding from the nasty mud of the unending plain. Perhaps I should not hope to convey in mere words the unutterable hideousness that can dwell in absolute silence and barren immensity. There was nothing within hearing, and nothing in sight save a vast reach of black slime; yet the very completeness of the stillness and the homogeneity of the landscape oppressed me with a nauseating fear.

The sun was blazing down from a sky which seemed to me almost black in its cloudless cruelty; as though reflecting the inky marsh beneath my feet. As I crawled into the stranded boat I realised that only one theory could explain my position. Through some unprecedented volcanic upheaval, a portion of the ocean floor must have been thrown to the surface, exposing regions which for innumerable millions of years had lain hidden under unfathomable watery depths. So great was the extent of the new land which had risen beneath me, that I could not detect the faintest noise of the surging ocean, strain my ears as I might. Nor were there any sea-fowl to prey upon the dead things.

For several hours I sat thinking or brooding in the boat, which lay upon its side and afforded a slight shade as the sun moved across the heavens. As the day progressed, the ground lost some of its stickiness, and seemed likely to dry sufficiently for travelling purposes in a short time. That night I slept but little, and the next day I made for myself a pack containing food and water, preparatory to an overland journey in search of the vanished sea and possible rescue.

On the third morning I found the soil dry enough to walk upon with ease. The odour of the fish was maddening; but I was too much concerned with graver things to mind so slight an evil, and set out boldly for an unknown goal. All day I forged steadily westward, guided by a far-away hummock which rose higher than any other elevation on the rolling desert. That night I encamped, and on the following day still travelled toward the hummock, though that object seemed scarcely nearer than when I had first espied it. By the fourth evening I attained the base of the mound, which turned out to be much higher than it had appeared from a distance; an intervening valley setting it out in sharper relief from the general surface. Too weary to ascend, I slept in the shadow of the hill.

I know not why my dreams were so wild that night; but ere the waning and fantastically gibbous moon had risen far above the eastern plain, I was awake in a cold perspiration, determined to sleep no more. Such visions as I had experienced were too much for me to endure again. And in the glow of the moon I saw how unwise I had been to travel by day. Without the glare of the parching sun, my journey would have cost me less energy; indeed, I now felt quite able to perform the ascent which had deterred me at sunset. Picking up my pack, I started for the crest of the eminence.

I have said that the unbroken monotony of the rolling plain was a source of vague horror to me; but I think my horror was greater when I gained the summit of the mound and looked down the other side into an immeasurable pit or canyon, whose black recesses the moon had not yet soared high enough to illumine. I felt myself on the edge of the world; peering over the rim into a fathomless chaos of eternal night. Through my terror ran curious reminiscences of *Paradise Lost*, and of Satan's hideous climb through the unfashioned realms of darkness.

As the moon climbed higher in the sky, I began to see that the slopes of the valley were not quite so perpendicular as I had imagined. Ledges and outcroppings of rock afforded fairly easy footholds for a descent, whilst after a drop of a few hundred feet, the declivity became very gradual. Urged on by an impulse which I cannot definitely analyse, I scrambled with difficulty down the rocks and stood on the gentler slope beneath, gazing into the Stygian deeps where no light had yet penetrated.

All at once my attention was captured by a vast and singular object on the opposite slope, which rose steeply about an hundred yards ahead of me; an object that gleamed whitely in the newly bestowed rays of the ascending moon. That it was merely a gigantic piece of stone, I soon assured myself; but I was conscious of a distinct impression that its contour and position were not altogether the work of Nature. A closer scrutiny filled me with sensations I cannot express; for despite its enormous magnitude, and its position in an abyss which had yawned at the bottom of the sea since the world was young, I perceived beyond a doubt that the strange object was a well-shaped monolith whose massive bulk had known the workmanship and perhaps the worship of living and thinking creatures.

Dazed and frightened, yet not without a certain thrill of the scientist's or archaeologist's delight, I examined my surroundings more closely. The moon, now near the zenith, shone weirdly and vividly above the towering steeps that hemmed in the chasm, and revealed the fact that a far-flung body of water flowed at the bottom, winding out of sight in both directions, and almost lapping my feet as I stood on the slope. Across the chasm, the wavelets washed the base of the Cyclopean monolith; on whose surface I could now trace both inscriptions and crude sculptures. The writing was in a system of hieroglyphics unknown to me, and unlike anything I had ever seen in books; consisting for the most part of conventionalised aquatic symbols such as fishes, eels, octopi, crustaceans, molluscs, whales, and the like. Several characters obviously represented marine things which are unknown to the modern world, but whose decomposing forms I had observed on the ocean-risen plain.

It was the pictorial carving, however, that did most to hold me spellbound. Plainly visible across the intervening water on account of their enormous size, were an array of bas-reliefs whose subjects would have excited the envy of a Doré. I think that these things were supposed to depict men—at least, a certain sort of men; though the creatures were shewn disporting like fishes in the waters of some marine grotto, or paying homage at some monolithic shrine which appeared to be under the waves as well. Of their faces and forms I dare not speak in detail; for the mere remembrance makes me grow faint. Grotesque beyond the imagination of a Poe or a Bulwer, they were damnably human in general outline despite webbed hands and feet, shockingly wide and flabby lips, glassy, bulging eyes, and other features less pleasant to recall. Curiously enough, they seemed to have been chiselled badly out of proportion with their scenic background; for one of the creatures was shewn in the act of killing a whale represented as but little larger than himself. I remarked, as I say, their grotesqueness and strange size; but in a moment decided that they were merely the imaginary gods of some primitive fishing or seafaring tribe; some tribe whose last descendant had perished eras before the first ancestor of the Piltdown or Neanderthal Man was born. Awestruck at this unexpected glimpse into a past beyond the conception of the most daring anthropologist, I stood musing whilst the moon cast queer reflections on the silent channel before me.

Then suddenly I saw it. With only a slight churning to mark its rise to the surface, the thing slid into view above the dark waters. Vast, Polyphemus-like, and loathsome, it darted like a stupendous monster of nightmares to the monolith, about which it flung its gigantic scaly arms, the while it bowed its hideous head and gave vent to certain measured sounds. I think I went mad then.

Of my frantic ascent of the slope and cliff, and of my delirious journey back to the stranded boat, I remember little. I believe I sang a great deal, and laughed oddly when I was unable to sing. I have indistinct recollections of a great storm some time after I reached the boat; at any rate, I know that I heard peals of thunder and other tones which Nature utters only in her wildest moods.

When I came out of the shadows I was in a San Francisco hospital; brought thither by the captain of the American ship which had picked up my boat in mid-ocean. In my delirium I had said much, but found that my words had been given scant attention. Of any land upheaval in the Pacific, my rescuers knew nothing; nor did I deem it necessary to insist upon a thing which I knew they could not believe. Once I sought out a celebrated ethnologist, and amused him with peculiar questions regarding the ancient Philistine legend of Dagon, the Fish-God; but soon perceiving that he was hopelessly conventional, I did not press my inquiries.

It is at night, especially when the moon is gibbous and waning, that I see the thing. I tried morphine; but the drug has given only transient surcease, and has drawn me into its clutches as a hopeless slave. So now I am to end it all, having written a full account for the information or the contemptuous amusement of my fellow-men. Often I ask myself if it could not all have been a pure phantasm—a mere freak of fever as I lay sun-stricken and raving in the open boat after my escape from the German man-of-war. This I ask myself, but ever does there come before me a hideously vivid vision in reply. I cannot think of the deep sea without shuddering at the nameless things that may at this very moment be crawling and floundering on its slimy bed, worshipping their ancient stone idols and carving their own detestable likenesses on submarine obelisks of water-soaked granite. I dream of a day when they may rise above the billows to drag down in their reeking talons the remnants of puny, war-exhausted mankind—of a day when the land shall sink, and the dark ocean floor shall ascend amidst universal pandemonium.

The end is near. I hear a noise at the door, as of some immense slippery body lumbering against it. It shall not find me. God, that hand! The window! The window!

H.P. Lovecraft is arguably the most important writer of horror fiction since Edgar Allen Poe. Lovecraft, a practitioner of what was at the time referred to as Weird Fiction, ripped open the possibilities of fantastic fiction in ways that are still being measured today. His Cthulhu mythos is literally the literary equivalent of splitting the atom. All dark fiction that followed owes an allegiance to Mr. Lovecraft's suffering and work. While it is true Mr. Lovecraft's social attitudes toward other cultures would not fly in contemporary times, it is important to note that he was a product of his era and, more importantly, his art is his only relevant contribution to the world. And what a contribution it has been! "Dagon" originally appeared in the eleventh issue of *The Vagrant*, in 1919. It was adapted for the screen by Stuart Gordon in 2001.

Thelemite

interview by Scotch Rutherford

Greek Heavy Metal band Thelemite has just released Powers of Darkness, a Dracula concept album loud enough to wake Bram Stoker from the dead. Scotch Rutherford sat down with the madmen from Athens for another conversation:

Members:
Yiannis: Guitars, Vocals, synth
Nikos: Bass
Zack: Guitars
Renos: Drums

SR: Guys welcome back. One more time for the readers... Who is Thelemite?

Nikos, Zack, Renos: Hi, thanks for having us, thanks for the invitation.

Yiannis: Thelemite is a heavy metal band from Athens, Greece. Founded in 2010, we count four released albums. Aleister Crowley is our godfather. Our vision has to do with keeping the flame alive, highlighting the all-time-classic key elements of our favorite music always with our own signature.

SR: What sparked a Dracula Concept Album?

Yiannis: While moving to the next stage off the pre-production process, several new songs were there, but still not an idea special enough to solidify the musical total conceptually, the "motto" of the album.

There were of course some

songs with a familiar kind of vampire & dark fantasy themes, but as a whole there wasn't actually something that could identify it for me. Then I decided that it was the right time to dedicate a night to research in order to come up with something that would do. It was the previous autumn to winter, that I was already a lot into Dracula/ pre-code silent horror stuff, and the new Nosferatu movie came out just on the right time to enhance the overall vibe. So while I was looking for info, vibing into a rather "gothic" season, I suddenly came across *Powers of Darkness* at Wikipedia! That was actually a lighting bulb moment for me! *Powers of Darkness* (Swedish: *Mörkrets makter*) was an anonymous 1899 Swedish adaptation of Bram's Stoker's 1897 novel *Dracula*. This reading downplays the vampirism of Stoker's novel and portrays Dracula primarily as the head of an international cult inspired by social Darwinism, new experimental trends that were fashionable at the dawn of the 20th century, when social and reli-gious movements set their ideologies under question. This single edition, which combines Stoker's gothic masterpiece, with the Darwinism of our previous "Survival of the Fittest" (2023) but also the occult, created the magic that connects our two releases thematically, filling me with inspiration...But also the feeling that everything happens for a reason, and that ...Crowley (our godfather), is watching us from somewhere that I can't explain at the moment and is rubbing his hands!

SR: I had no idea that book existed. Fascinating. So, there was some inspiration from the 2024 Robert Eggers' film *Nosferatu*?

Yiannis: Totally! It added vibes, the timing was great. Aesthetically we draw a lot of inspiration off this.

Renos: I think that the reference in our newly de-signed logo is pretty clear.

S.R: There seems to be a lot of themes of the supernatural and the occult in your work. Have horror films been a big influence on Thelemite?

Renos: I love supernatural and horror movies

Zack: I think it is a subconscious thing, due to the fact that we love such kind of themes.

Yiannis: Sure they've been. Actually they are important to the evolution of our own art. Everything in inspiration as I always repeat has to do with the vibes, the atmosphere. And then the magic happens. The impact that these classics played a great role and the proof is "POD." We are very proud of not only having the feeling of belonging to this culture, but also that we motivate people to search themselves for knowledge through these masterpieces such as the work of Stoker or even the cryptic writings of Crowley. After all, we're always an occult-inspired project. Black & white 20-30's German expressionism films, gothic movies, and occult-dark fantasy themes, excites us.

SR: Which one was better… *Dracula* (1931) or *Nosferatu* (1922)?

Yiannis: I can't decide because both are fundamental to the gothic horror genre and fash-ion. We are talking about two historic releases that defined a lot of things through the following century and influenced a real lot not only in cinema but also everywhere. Bela Lugosi as Dracula by Tom Browning, and Max Schreck as Nosferatu by F.W. Murnau. I even get chills spelling these names. *Nosferatu*, was also an unlicensed movie, same as the *Powers of Darkness* book was. Crazy thing about that is that Ms. Stoker sued the production and won the case. Every copy was destroyed, but the only one that survived lived to tell the tale, and so they put their mark forever! So don't tell me that something darker was going on haha. My favorite Dracula is of course Coppola's 1992 film, as we know that by "Night of the Wolf" already, and I have to say Egger's *Nosferatu* was quite a decent effort.

S.R: Yeah, for sure. The Coppola film's influence is undeniable. The music video for "Night of the Wolf" was fantastic. Any music videos in the works for "Powers of Darkness"?

Renos, Zack, Nikos: Thanks! Thanks a lot.

Yiannis: Thank you very much, what can I say, you already honored us with Die Laughing, and we will be forever grateful for this. Of course it was something like the little brother of 1992's *Dracula*, dipped in some heavy metal! We are preparing a video for "Waiting for the Night", so you guys are the first to know! As you might suspect, it will be directed in an appropriate gothic scenery which we will reveal real soon.

S.R: Are you guys touring this year? If so, where?

Nikos: We will play for the first time outside Greece, at Varna, Vulgaria!

Renos: And I will be the lucky driver to the destination haha!

Yiannis: We will do Varna at August 30.

Zack: I hope you don't hold the map upside down!

Yiannis: And do you wanna know what's special about that destination? "Demeter", the ship that carried Dracula's boxes of soil, and had all its crew massacred by the beast, sailed from Varna to London! And then back to Varna again in order to take the train to Transylvania, when he had to return to his castle, weak from his London monstrous activities! Do you still believe it's a coincidence? I mean it's the first live of the tour and it happened just because it's the first offer we have! No kidding!

Zack: Oh no, they already had one Dracula, now they 're also gonna get HIM! (shows Yiannis)

SR: What's you guys' dream concert venue? (if you could play anywhere) Waken, Hellfest, M3?

Yiannis: Hmmm that's a nice question. Maybe opening for Savatage, or something like that.

Renos: I'd love to play at Ziggo Dome, Netherlands.

Nikos: Luzhniki Olympic Sport Complex Moscow (Ozzy, Metallica, Scorpions), with Putin at the VIP seats, sporting a blonde Dave Mustaine wig (according to the meme)!!!

Zack: Long Beach Arena, Iron Maiden, Live after Death, 1984!

SR: Wow, a lot of variety in those answers! What's next for Thelemite?

Nikos: We are booking the next shows of the tour right now, in order to promote the album, basically with the additional help of our manager Tolis, who is also the boss of our record company, Sleaszy Rider records.

Renos: We are excited about that, can't wait to meet our new friends and fans, we'll do our best to give a great show each and every time.

Yiannis: Thank you very much for having us, *Pulp Modern* Special thanks to you, Scotch. Always there for us, you are part of the family. You're the man!

SR: Aw, thanks, brother. It's an honor. Best of fortunes to you all on the 2025 tour.

Thelemite is a Heavy Metal horde of axe-and-sticks-wielding heathens from Athens whose sole purpose is to conquer the stage like the rock gods of yore and return this world to the age of classic Metal. Their albums "Powers of Darkness" and "Survival of the Fittest" are now available from Sleazy Rider Records.

An unbelievable monstrosity towered over him.

Hell Hole

adapted by J.D. Graves
based on a script by Gregory Shultz

Mason did a terrible thing. Even twenty years later, he could still smell the burning hair and hear Keith's agonized screams. When you're fifteen, the future is limitless—like a dream—something far off and constantly floating away. A type of object permanence in a perpetual state of arrested development. At that age, when accidents happen, it's seen as the cost of doing business. Until the punk ages into adulthood where the stakes rise too high to justify errors. Big if true, he thought.

Country music twang'd from the Bronco's dashboard as Mason doodled in the margins of an instruction manual. Humming along with the music, letting his mind drag out the past like a boulder on a chain. To distract himself, he scribbled imagery from Dr. Strangelove. Slim Pickens yee-hawing a nuke to its fi-nal destination. Kaboom! World War III erupts to some bird singing about meeting again. *"Don't know where—don't know when."* However, Mason's line art of Captain 'King' Kong rode the bomb just over a paragraph on how to properly inspect control modules.

Bad luck and trouble were Mason's only friends these days. A tumultuous lawsuit for negligence will do that to people. Mason felt a twinge of guilt creep in. He knew it was best to keep a clear head while out on the job trying your best to hide from doing any real work. And the Bisbee Weapons Research Facility

didn't lack for hiding places. The craggy compound looked desolate. Roads cut zig-zags through and around boulders, cliff faces, and mounds of rock. Mason could stand on the Bronco's roof and still see nothing but endless Arizona rock. The gig paid next to nothing but offered its scrub employees hours of contemplation. Some of the old timers said it was the only fringe benefit. The extended time for meandering thought did Mason no good. He knew there was no going back. Once did, somethings can't be undid.

Everything in Mason's life changed the moment his ex-buddy Keith stepped inside that gasoline-soaked barricade and lit the wet cardboard.

Whoosh!

Mason! His walkie-talkie interrupted the bad trip down memory lane. **Do you copy, over?**

He looked up from his instruction manual and the scenes from Kubrick movies. Fingers fumbled for the ancient two way, "Yeah control right here."

What is your twenty, you still checking those tags?

"Ugh," Mason thought quick, "just a few more to go."

Static screamed in his palm, **All right then get after it!**

He'd been pinched and knew it. Offered his boss a meek, "Copy that."

He sighed with disappointment, tossed the instruction manual into the passenger seat, and twisted the starter of the '78 Ford Bronco.

Motor roared to life. Headlights cut through the Arizona dusk as Mason dropped the lever lurching the old beast onto the gravel trail. Soon enough, a concrete silo rose from the rocks, speckled with powerlines. The "research" tower was one of many that dotted the facility for miles around. Mason stopped outside the large cargo door. Debris piled on the Bronco's floorboard. Hand swirled around the mess until fingers found the gate opener. *Click-click.*

The cargo door yawned wide enough a Zeppelin could float through. Mason banished the controller back into the messy abyss and toed the accelerator. Just as the Bronco passed, the heavy door squealed closed.

Down Mason drove into

the winding darkness of the 'research' silo.

The gig wasn't hard, just not something he wanted to do. The facility owned eleven hundred fire extinguishers and each one needed its tag checked. The Bronco stopped beside a concrete pillar. The door squealing and groaning as Mason stepped out. Jacket sleeve rubbed a layer of dust from the canister's gauge—needle still green zoned. Tamper seal verified un-broken. Pin remained securely in place. Other than a few superficial cracks at the very tip of the nozzle, the thing passed inspection. As he lifted the heavy thing from its hook, thoughts of Keith returned.

If only he'd had access to one of these extinguishers all of them years ago, maybe he wouldn't be having to inspect them now. Big if true, he thought. Maybe his folks wouldn't have been sued into financial ruin. Even bigger, Mason smiled. Maybe Mason could've accepted that scholar-ship and be out in Hollywood making miniatures for movies instead of just dreaming about it. This sudden acute case of the 'may-be's' reserved one more

for him. The absolute biggest, Mason's face dimmed. Mason winced as he thought, maybe Keith wouldn't have endured countless skin grafts and still be his best friend. Flames so hot, the boy's tears evaporated from his crying eyes.

Mason shuddered.

Maybe he shouldn't waste his time thinking about such things.

Mason made note of the extinguisher's weight and got back in the Bronco.

He drove on.

Mason didn't rightly know the silo's total depth. The further down you drove the colder it got. Breath fogged in the dashboard light. Down here, amongst the forever night of a mile below ground, the shadows could play tricks on you—noises and strange shapes and roads suddenly ending without warning.

The Bronco's brakes squealed. Headlights illumin-ated the words: **NO WAY OUT**. Mason shifted into reverse. Brake lights glowed red against the rock walls behind him as he straightened out the whip and drove on.

"Easy to get turned around down here," Mason chuckled.

Rumor in town whispered the only research happening out here was housing US nuclear ordinance. Big if true, Mason thought. It made as much sense as anything if you thought about it. Hence all the extinguishers. Mason chuckled again at his own cleverness. As if nuclear fallout could be extinguished so easily. Mason guffawed as he pictured the end of Dr. Strangelove. Mushroom clouds sprouting across the horizon. Keith screaming for his mama.

Wait a second…Mason shook his head to clear it.

Low noise rumbled from somewhere deep. The Bronco quaked. Silo settling again, he thought. It happened sporadically in all the ones Mason serviced. Control informed him not to worry since it was out of his paygrade. And since Mason had so much other shit clogging his noggin he followed those orders to the letter.

After five or six more canisters his comm chirped. **Mason!**

"Go ahead control."

The comm barked out orders. **The rails in chamber 19 need a fresh coat of paint.**

Mason's blood ran cold. "Chamber 19?"

Control's garbled voice instructed him to enter and start repainting the staircase railings. Inspection was past due and if they found the place lacking in routine maintenance, the company would lose funding.

"But those platforms are a hundred feet above… above…" Mason hesitated to name it. The end of Dr. Strangelove sprang to mind. "Who knows what kind of nuclear armaments y'all got hiding down below!"

Control cut him off, **We don't do that here**. More static. **This is a research facility. Now get in there and get the job done!**

Mason inquired about PPE and could almost hear the laughter through the static.

To paint a railing? Control said. **You do not need personal protective equipment for this gig!**

Mason said nothing as Keith's agonized screams echoed off the walls and rattled inside his head.

Control cautioned. **This place is covered in Lead-based paint! It chips and** contaminates the research chambers! You gotta keep it covered or else there will be hell to pay!

Next thing Mason knew he'd stopped the Bronco outside a metal door protruding from the rock. Chamber 19 painted overhead along with a strange hieroglyph. Somewhere between warnings for both nuclear and biohazardous material and Mason wasn't sure what it meant exactly. It too was above his paygrade.

Metal on metal screeched as he pulled the door closed behind him. Temperature-wise felt cold enough to burn. Breath fogged over his shoulder as he found the paint bucket and stepped onto the grated platform. Mason kept his eyes straight ahead. No need to glance down or up. The silo's size neared impossible in both directions—as if carved into the Earth by gods to keep their secrets safe. Nethers jellied and quaked as he neared the edge of the platform. Chipped yellow paint crusted on the guardrail. It flaked off as he touched it. Falling all the way down to a closed hexagon floor portal. If someone fell from here, they might survive and wish they hadn't. Mason swallowed the lump in his throat. Slowly knelt, focusing his attention on the beat-up paint can.

No paint key could be found, so he fished for the Bronco's and dug in. Whichever son-of-a-bitch used it last left it damned mess. Mason carved away the dried yellow. Swore under his breath as the Bronco's key found a gap. It took some doing, but the thing finally released. Mason gagged. A stink somewhere between rotten eggs and spoilt varnish fouled the silo's air. A yellow mass floated on milky water. "Damn," Mason said and pocketed the Bronco's keys—produced a screwdriver and stabbed the rubbery cake. Sweat beaded on his forehead as chunks rippled. Yellow splattered everywhere. Eventually, it separated enough to resemble something like paint.

Mason sat the can on the railing for easier access. Dipped in the brush. Spread the nasty on top of the nasty and whistled as he worked.

His mind wandered.

Keith returned.

Moments before it happened, he'd been happy and smiling and wearing a fluffy pink clown wig. The things kids will do to impress their friends for a class presentation. Building the barricade had taken all day. Keith's mom would be picking him up in an hour, so they needed it to be spectacular in a hurry. The gasoline was all Keith's idea. Or was it? All these years later he couldn't remember exactly. But the fact was that Keith had memorized a speech. He was going to get inside the barricade of cardboard, start talking about social studies, then light it up and dance as the thing burned around him. With this much effort the boys were sure their teacher would reward them with at least a B plus. Mason's part was to press record on the camera. He did his part. But for some reason, Keith forgot the order of events. Once inside the barricade he immediately struck a match.

Whoosh!

Mason! Control grated over the radio. It gave Mason a bad jolt. His left elbow jerked a little, barely nudging the paint bucket on the railing. Time slowed. Just as it did all of them years ago.

Fire instantly igniting the gasoline fumes.

Paint bucket spun slightly then teetered over.

Cardboard instantly engulfed in flames.

Lid and bucket and screwdriver dropped a hundred feet down.

Mason stood slack-jawed, watching both tragedies unfold.

Keith screamed in agony as the paint bucket crashed into a control module below.

Glass shattered. Electricity popped. Sparks jumped.

Again, the radio crackled.

"Copy?" Mason responded in disbelief.

Alarm bells deafened. Their hellish noise echoed off the silo's metal walls. Red light glowed. The hexagon floor portal split open. Heat rose in angry waves. Now, a bottomless red abyss stared directly up at Mason.

Mason we got big problems what is your twenty?

Mason couldn't believe his eyes.

Mason do you copy?

Panic seized his mind.

Something in the fiery abyss

below growled, then moved. The silo shook.

It moved again.

Mason slammed the Bronco's door closed. Fumbled for the keys. Jammed on the starter. Cranked the lever in reverse. Tires spun gravel in all directions as Mason twisted the wheel. Earth shook around him. Dust fell in heavy clouds from the tunnel's ceiling. Mason flicked on the wipers to clear it. He drove like a mad bastard. Fist slamming repeatedly against the Bronco's roof overhead. Each punch accentuated with, "No! No! No! No!"

Mason! Do you copy?

He grabbed the comm, "Um...just needed a new battery...um I'm going to finish painting the..."

Control cut him off, **You gotta get out of there!**

"Um...is it a missile launch or something?"

More static, **You fool! That is not what goes on here!**

The comm went dead. Mason threw it aside and kept driving. Road ahead split. Mason couldn't remember which path was which. Hand over hand veered the Bronco to the left—immediate regret. At first, he thought he saw brake lights. As if another vehicle was down here with him. Sweat ran down the side of his face. The chill from earlier, long gone. Temperature rose steadily.

"That's not brake lights," Mason said.

It sure wasn't.

The Bronco slowed to a dead end wall shimmering with heat. Stone glowed the deepest crimson he'd seen since pulling Keith's burned body from the fire. A low growl rattled around the Bronco.

The comm bristled with garbled static. He picked it up and spoke slow, "Control? There's something strange happening down here."

Control didn't answer.

It never would again.

One of the glowing red rocks cracked.

Mason watched the pebbles fall like a child mesmerized by a magician's trick. Then...

Boom!

It happened so fast. Rock and debris exploded in all directions. Peppering the Bronco and cracking the windshield. Through

the dust a monstrous claw emerged. Mason screamed as it snapped over the Bronco's hood. Mason thought quick. Hand reversed gears. Eyes unable to look away from the enormous pincer opening and closing where the Bronco had just been. Didn't see the **Do Not Enter** sign as the Bronco slammed through guardrails and into a backhoe.

Mason's heart raced.

Switched into drive and floored it.

Motor revved but didn't move.

Tachometer redlined.

Wheels spun.

Claw inched closer. He could see it was lined with teeth. Each snap sounded like breaking bones. Dashboard illuminated with warning signs. For a moment, Mason knew it was over. His life didn't flash before his eyes though. Just the panicked face of Keith as the pink clown wig melted to his skull.

Mason's hand dropped the gear shift into low. The motor screamed. He heard a pop. Then a metallic clang as the bumper fell free. The Bronco lunged toward the advancing claw. At the last second, he spun the wheel averting another collision.

All around the charging Bronco everything shook.

Speedometer needle hovered over sixty-five.

A concrete pillar passed. Then another. And another. Soon Mason knew he'd be at the gate.

"Shit!" Mason said, "The gate!"

Immediately his right hand began searching the floorboard.

"Where is it?" He cried. "Where?"

Snack wrappers, instruction manuals, and other garbage tossed aside as his search grew more frantic. Finally— paydirt.

Mason looked up just in time to see a solid wall rushing into focus.

He screamed. Foot stomped on the parking brake. Tires locked. Steering wheel pressed into Mason's chest. He swerved. Bronco's right side met rock wall with a terrible crunch. Mason released the parking brake and floored it. Bronco scraped along the wall then moved further away.

The closed gate waited ahead. His thumb mashed

the button in desperation. The metal barrier opened slowly. He didn't want to slow down. Didn't want to wait for it to open. *Clack-Clack!* The passenger side-mirror broke off as the Bronco raced through.

Relief, although momentary, washed over him. He brought the Bronco to a stop outside the gate. He rolled the window down to let the Arizona night air clear his head. His heart galloped in his chest. Had this really happened? Big if true, he thought.

A terrible growl shook the world. The silo above burst open. Flaming rock rained down. And Mason saw it. An unbelievable monstrosity towered over him. A thing, somewhere between a crab and a minotaur loomed over the escaping Bronco. Mason didn't wait around for a better look. What he saw was enough to plague him for the rest of his miserable life. And whatever bellowed loudly into the sky seemed ancient and older than man itself. It's body scarred and scabby as if suffering third degree burns from head to toe. Just like…

Mason drove and drove and drove, but he knew there would be no escape.

Keith bellowed as tens of Blackhawks opened fire.

Mason couldn't watch it happen—not again. Not after all these years. He couldn't bring himself to *yee-haw* this bombshell. Tears streamed down his cheeks, as a new terrible truth was unleashed on the world.

Mason had done a terrible thing, once again.

J.D. Graves is an award winning filmmaker, and indie author of MAYHEM SAM a splatter western novel published by Death's Head Press. His play TALL PINES LODGE was an official selection of the New York International Fringe Festival and FronteraFEST respectively. Films produced have programmed across the US with CAPTIVE MARKET recently having its West Coast premiere as an official selection of the Newport Beach Film Festival. J.D. continues to write and live in the woods of East Texas with his wife and family.

PROJECT N-TERRO

A tortured agent dives into
a trafficker's mind using a
banned psychic drug—
what she finds isn't just
evidence, it's her own
past rewritten.

KQPictures presents a Monique Efta film "Project N-terro"
Starring David Nett, Courtney Merritt, Paula Rhodes, & Traycee King
Written by Traycee King Produced by Traycee King & Stephanie Thorpe

Being the angel of death was thirsty work.

Croak

adapted by Sarah Cannavo
from the script written by Matt Barrett

The creak of the screen door opening reached Jimmy even over the music spilling through his headphones, and after considering whether it was worth the effort he lazily raised his sunglasses and looked toward the porch without bothering to shift position on the couch he lounged on—which had been on the back lawn so long even he couldn't remember who'd dragged it out there in the first place—as Todd emerged from the house carrying what *had* to be, by now, the last box of his crap.

"All right, sooo I cleaned up the kitchen and trimmed up the front a little bit, so that should be it." Todd stopped on the porch's edge, resting the box on the railing and patting it as if uncertain what else to do. Jimmy said nothing, did nothing, cigarette still smoldering between the fingers of his right hand as he stared at his soon-to-be-former roommate, who put his hands on his hips and stared back, as if expecting Jimmy to toss confetti and kiss the bearded traitor's ass for putting the Cap'n Crunch back in the pantry and whacking a few weeds on his way out.

Screw that, buddy. Jimmy blew a slow cloud of smoke, giving the barest nod he could. "Mm-hmm."

"You can keep that grass whip if you want; Jessica has weed-eater that we're gonna use."

Oooh, really, the grass whip? All mine? Well damn, looks like Santa came early this year. And a hell of way to top off that pitiful peace offering, mentioning Jessica like that—

Jessica who, the few times she'd deigned to come over, looked like she'd stepped in something whenever Jimmy was around and kept making not-so-subtle comments about the state of the lawn, the abundant piles of PawPaw's bottles, and the place's general...*musk*, as Jimmy liked to call it, which, if she'd bothered to try a little harder, she probably would've just gotten used to, the way he had. When she'd started making more and more such comments and Todd mounted less and less of a defense, Jimmy had suspected something was up, but hadn't thought it would ever actually come to *this*, a nice fat grass whip right up the ass from a guy he'd thought was his friend.

Well, he wasn't going to smile and thank the bastard for it, that was for damn sure. Expression unchanged, he brought his cigarette back to his lips and said flatly, stretching the words out, "Oh, awesome."

Something seemed to snap in Todd then, exasperation reigning as he said, "Listen, man, I know it's early. I'm *sorry*. I just...I can't do this anymore. This place is like a swamp."

Jimmy hadn't wanted to engage; if Todd was so desperate to abandon him, he could just *go*. But he also wasn't about to stand—okay, sit—here and let some false history get written, either. "Okay," he said, and he sounded a bit cranky even to his own ears now, but really, who the hell could blame him? "I said that I would clean it up, and I'm just—I'm just really tired!"

"You're always tired, Jimmy," Todd replied without a drop of sympathy.

"What is so wrong about the way I'm doing things?" Jimmy demanded. "I have a job, I pay my end of the bills—"

"You pay the *bills*?!"

Anger flared supernova-hot behind Jimmy's eyes, anger and a bone-deep pang of bitter pain that hit him even harder, as if Todd had just jammed his thumb into a fresh bruise he himself had given Jimmy, adding insult to injury. What right did Todd have to take that tone with him, like he was just some random asshole off the street and not a guy he'd known for years, a guy he'd partied just as hard as before deciding some buttoned-up, IKEA-bought lifestyle was the better way to go and anyone who didn't agree was some lesser creature it was okay to look down on, no matter the friends they'd been before?

No way would he let Todd see how upset he was, though, now or ever; anger was safer, easier. Stabbing his finger at him he spat, "Fuck you, Todd, okay; they get paid either way," sucking down another lungful of smoke to punctuate the point.

Todd didn't say a word, just picked up his box and turned away, and Jimmy felt a small bright core of smug satisfaction bloom in his chest. *What, all out of lectures, dude?*

But he shouldn't have challenged the universe like that, because Todd swung around again and started down the porch steps saying, "You know, man, I don't wanna leave," setting the box on the bottom of the railing and resting his arm atop it as he reached the last step. "We've had a lot of fun here. But we both knew this would eventually happen. Please don't make this harder than it has to be, okay? Let's end on a good note, and...I'll come back tomorrow and help you clean this up."

A small voice in the back of Jimmy's mind, thin and wispy as the smoke trailing up from his cigarette, whispered *Say okay*, and as he considered the offer he thought he caught a flash of hope in Todd's face that this last-ditch olive branch of his was working, that maybe things between them weren't quite as irrevocably fucked-up as they'd seemed— as he'd made them.

Say okay, the voice urged him again, and when he opened his mouth the words popped out as fully-formed and perfect as that hot naked Greek-goddess chick riding the shell out of the sea in all those old-ass paintings.

"Can you, uh, can you teach me how to tie my shoes, too?"

This time Todd was definitely done, hefting the box and heading back up the stairs with a disgusted "Okay."

"No, I'm serious!" Jimmy called after him.

"See you tomorrow, Jimmy."

"I don't know whether the rabbit follows, or whether it leads!"

Todd offered no retort or reply as he vanished inside the house—in the old days he would've given it right back to Jimmy, called him an asshole or flipped him the bird at least, but that, like everything and everyone else lately, was probably beneath him now, too—and Jimmy slouched back against the couch with another angry drag on the cigarette, muttering "Fucking bastard" into the gloom of the afternoon. The screen door swung shut and Jimmy exhaled another long column of smoke toward the sky, disappointed that the door hadn't actually hit Todd on the ass on his way out.

Go then, dude. We'll see who's sorry first.

They started with the darkness, as always, a chorus of croaks rising from the backyard until it seemed they were in the room with him, ringed around the bed where they were keeping him sleepless once again. Closing the window only muffled the bastards—not to mention made the room hot as balls with the freaking A/C on the fritz again—and Jimmy rolled onto his back, twisted in his sheets and exhaling heavily as he stared up at the ceiling in the moonlit dimness. He'd tried counting sheep, like Nana had always suggested when he couldn't sleep as a kid, but by the fourth or fifth they turned into frogs without fail, stupid little green-black frogs that hopped over imaginary fence-posts with cartoonish ease, croaking all the while. If he wanted to get to sleep before his alarm blared in the morning, it was going to take something stronger.

Sorry, Nana. Rolling to his right Jimmy reached over to his nightstand, past the piles of crumpled cigarette packs, to the cluster of brown PawPaw's bottles, fishing until he found one that looked most likely to have a little left inside and swirling it around, listening for the telltale swish. Nothing—God, it really wasn't his night—but in desperation he turned it over anyway, when nothing magically came spilling out dropping it to the floor with a dull crack of glass.

To top it off the goddamn frogs were still going, croaking their little amphibian hearts out, and the fiery pressure that'd been simmering in his skull all night mounted with every ribbit until it felt like his brain was going to burst, come leaking out his ears like the foam of a shaken beer; rolling onto his stomach Jimmy buried his face in his pillow and screamed long and loud, but it didn't help much, mostly served to reinforce how dry his throat was.

To the fridge then, blinking in the yellow glare of its light as he grabbed one of the bottles from the back and slammed the door shut again. For a moment he considered heading back to bed, but the thought of lying there sweating and sleepless—and not in a fun way—made his skin crawl, so he settled his headphones over his ears and chose the back porch instead, bottle in one hand and a cigarette in the other; he'd hear those damn frogs either way, but at least there'd be fresh air out there.

The music tried, but the frogs' voices still filtered through as Jimmy breathed out smoke and stared across the dark yard, doing his best to think about nothing like those meditation freaks always babbled about, to no great effect.

Screw them, then. Screw them, and Mr. "I'll-come-back-tomorrow," and screw that asshole Bob at work for good measure, and—as an especially piercing croak reached him over the music—*SCREW THESE FUCKING FROGS.*

He chugged the last few mouthfuls and threw the bottle into the overflow of its brethren in the recycling bin, the impact dislodging something that fell to the ground with a clatter: the grass whip Todd had so graciously left behind, Jimmy saw, smoking as he stared at it, remembering, contemplating, before slowly reaching down and picking it up. Something started to bubble in his brain at the weight and solidity of it in his hand, as he ran his gaze along the black teeth grinning at the end of it, and as the frogs' voices reached him again he snapped his head toward the back lawn, fingers tightening on the handle.

He moved without thinking into the yard, grass whip held high. *"Fucking flysuckers, shut the fuck up!"*

But they evidently didn't know what was good for them, because they *didn't* shut up, and he couldn't stand it a second longer, blind rage filling him as he glimpsed one of the fuckers sitting in the grass like it didn't have a care in the world until down came the grass whip, a warm spray of blood erupting into the humid night air, and *God*, it felt good, it felt *great*, better than any high he'd ever been on.

Who's next, huh? Who's next who's next WHO'S NEXT?

Splat—crunch—squish. He was carnage incarnate as he charged through the yard, bringing the grass whip down on every frog he could find; he was the angel of death, he was Thor swinging the hammer of the fucking gods, he was the goddamn Coyote finally sinking his teeth into that mocking sonofabitch Road Runner, and there was nothing those asshole frogs could do about it but fucking *die*, blood bursting from small green bodies as the grass whip hit home again and again and again….

He only paused the slaughter for as long as it took to run back into the house and raid the fridge for more Paw-Paw's—being the angel of death was thirsty work, it turned out, but that was okay, because it *also* turned out to be fun as hell to launch an empty across the yard and nail Kermit like he had a fucking bulls-eye painted on his warty back. Time passed in quick snapshots, moments standing out amid the booze-and-adrenaline-blurred orgy of violence; he wasn't sure how many frogs he'd killed, or how many times he'd gone back to pillage his stash—he had a vague memory of falling once before the open mouth of the fridge, but he'd soldiered on and made it back outside intact for more slashing and bashing, his green tie-dye PARTY TIL YOU DIE T-shirt soaked with sweat and the foam that slopped from the bottles clutched in his increasingly-unsteady hand.

"Thanks for the grass whip, Jessica," he slurred as he stumbled around searching for stragglers, and when his bleary gaze couldn't find any he threw his arms into the air, savoring his victory for a few sweet seconds until his legs finally gave way and he passed out backward onto the porch, slipping into sleep so quickly he didn't catch the faint croaks still rising in the distant darkness.

Sunlight warm on his skin, the cheerful chirping of birds in the trees, his hand shoved comfortably beneath the waistband of his shorts; for a blissful moment Jimmy was aware only of the peace of the morning before the thunder of his hangover burst at his temples, bringing with it a lightning bolt that shocked his eyes open wide and his body upright on the leaf-and-bottle-strewn porch: He was late for work.

Again.

The plant loomed, a pale gray tangle of metal walls and towers, on the outskirts of town; most days Jimmy struggled to remember just what they did there, exactly—hell, most days he struggled to remember just what *he* did there, exactly. But today he was sure he knew just what stink-face the foreman would have when Bob saw him rolling up this late, and when he finally made it in,

the squeal of the delivery-bay door scraping down his spine, and fought his way past the tangle of chains that hung near the entrance like a cat battling his way out of a ball of yarn to where Bob was inspecting the latest shipment, he saw he'd at least been right about *that*.

"I am so sick of this shit," Bob informed him, slapping his clipboard down on one of the drums he'd been looking over and sounding way too much like Jimmy's mother had before he'd moved out. "I am, really."

The pink tie the foreman had, for reasons known only to God, chosen to leave the house in this morning wasn't doing anything good for Jimmy's pounding head, and neither was the glint of the fluorescent lights off the crown of Bob's head, but he managed to force out, "Bob, I'm sorry, I'm sorry, it's not my fault. The...The...The frogs—"

Bob held his hands up. "Enough." Adopting the voice of a movie-screen frat bro he said, "Party's over, dude," switching back to Big Tough Boss Bob to add, "I'm gonna need the uniform."

What? "Okay, you can't do that." Wasn't Bob *listening*? It was the fucking frogs' fault, and this clown was gonna *fire* him for it? The plant was still standing, for God's sake; nothing had exploded or melted down because he hadn't been here promptly at nine, and *he had a reason this time*, didn't that fucking count for *anything*?

"*I'm just really tired!*"

"*You're always tired, Jimmy.*"

"It's clear you have no desire to evolve here," Bob said, unmoved, "so you can go become someone else's burden."

The industrial buzz announcing another delivery sawed through Jimmy's skull, his mouth setting in a tight line against both the pain and Bob's power trip, staring the foreman down and waiting for him to buckle, sigh *Fine, whatever, stay on, but this is your last goddamn warning, I swear*, when he didn't turning and starting to walk away to heap some more pressure on.

At his back Bob called, "Hey, if you want your last paycheck, I'm gonna need that uniform."

Fuck, he *was* serious. Fine— he didn't need this shit job anyway. *Oh, you don't?* that back-of-the-mind voice from yesterday resurfaced to ask, but he buried it now as he had then, because if he hadn't let on how upset he really was to a guy who'd been his friend he sure as hell wasn't going to to a boss he'd been at war with from day one. Fingers fumbling to undo the buttons they'd done up as he'd raced out the front door, Jimmy slid off the baggy khaki work shirt, leaving himself in his black undershirt, and whipped it over to Bob, who caught it and looked at it as if it were an animal he didn't want to touch too long. Jimmy stormed off without looking back, the last word exchanged between the pair floating lowly in the air of the bay.

"Bitch."

Jimmy shoved his sunglasses back on and pulled a cigarette from his pocket as he pounded down the concrete steps and across the parking lot, sure he probably looked a little loony-tunes as he gestured and made wordless noises of frustration but not giving much of a fuck at the moment. Besides, the lot was empty, at least of people; a black delivery vehicle was parked at the other end and he made his weaving way toward it as he ran a hand through his thick sandy hair and took a drag—it was a van, not Bob's face, but it would have to do for now, he thought, giving the back door a short hard punch with his free hand and immediately regretting it, pain flaring from his knuckles up his arm.

"Ah, *fuck*," he spat, shaking his hand out, pulling his sunglasses off and ignoring the sunlight's sting as he assessed the damage. There didn't seem to be any, just another ache for his body to haul around, and he took another drag, leaning back against the rear of the van, only to jolt off with a low exclamation of surprised pain as a brief sizzling sound gave way to a throbbing burn high on his left arm.

The sun, he figured through his shock, heating the van like a metal playground slide in summer. But it wasn't a burn he saw when he looked, at least, not a normal hot-metal burn; a small irregular patch of skin seemed to have melted away completely, blood oozing from the wound in bright tendrils and the pain pulsing like electrical charges through his arm.

What the fuck could do *that*? Slowly he turned to the black van and tested the rear door, surprised when it slid open without complaint— oh, Bob was gonna be *pissed* at whoever was supposed to lock it up—and when he saw it hadn't been unloaded yet and what it was carrying he couldn't help but laugh, lowly and maniacally, all thought and pain of his hangover, his firing, his wound swept away by his rising glee.

Containers, dozens of them, all bearing the biohazard signs from every outbreak movie he'd ever seen, skull-and-crossbones labels shrieking DANGEROUS CHEMICALS, screaming E N V I R O N M E N T A L HAZARD with sketches of dead fish beneath the block letters, and Jimmy kept laughing as he looked over the gold mine—*his* gold mine—and as he laughed he stared at the dead fish gaping with black Xs for eyes and wondered how well his newfound treasure would work on creatures of a different kind.

Only one way to find out.

He donned a pair of yellow rubber gloves, a medical mask, and safety goggles that tinted the world yellow-green before he started, so at least nobody could accuse him of being unsafe as he whipped up a cocktail of the DANGEROUS CHEMICALS he'd lifted from work in a tall beaker on the kitchen island that night, watching the mix bubble and foam into a phosphorescent-green concoction straight out of a cartoon witch's cauldron.

Once the hissing mix settled somewhat, still glowing scifi green, he put the next stage of his plan into action, keeping his protective gear on and carrying a large plastic jar as he leapt from the porch into the backyard, digging through the brush Todd had always been on his ass to trim. *Come on, you bastard, come on…* He would've liked to think he'd gotten all the frogs in his blitz last night, but they'd infested the yard for so long he knew for every one he'd killed there were probably two more waiting to take their place, and—

"Gotcha!" His gloved hand closed around one that hopped a second too late, the feel of its rubbery body squirming frantically in his grip so disgusting he almost dropped it before he recovered and thrust it into the jar, screwing the lid shut and cutting off its croaked pleas as he raced back to the house. It let out another forlorn ribbit as Jimmy thumped the jar down on the island and dipped the large syringe he'd also snagged into the bubbling beaker, drawing the plunger back until the syringe was over half-full, and then it started pawing helplessly at the plastic walls of its prison, as if aware the end was near. Jimmy couldn't keep the laughter back again, the same low, manic laughter from the parking lot, as he watched the frog scrabble, picking the jar up and poising the loaded syringe above it.

Adios, motherf—

The kitchen doorknob squeaked as it turned, and he looked up to see Todd entering. *Oh. Right.* In light of recent developments, he'd completely forgotten Todd's charitable promise to "come back tomorrow" and help clean the place up.

"Jimmy." Todd's gaze slid to the jar he was holding, the glowing green syringe in his hand, the mess of chemical containers on the counter where they'd always dumped their junk mail. "Oh, God."

Jimmy gestured wordlessly—*what do you want?* Todd shook his head, and at the sight, at everything his expression implied, Jimmy felt that pressed-bruise pang of pain again, sharp and sore, in the hollow of his chest. "Don't you say—" He pulled his muffling mask off and tossed it down, pointing the syringe at his ex-roommate. "Don't you say anything, okay. I don't want to hear a word from you, okay." Todd kept staring, and Jimmy pressed on, the words boiling up like the mixture had climbed in the beaker, "You're always saying 'Hey, hey, do something around the house'—well, this is it." He shook the syringe a bit in emphasis. "This is what I'm doing. I'm shutting the goddamn frogs up." He grinned, pleased with himself.

Todd, evidently, was not. "*What?!*"

Jimmy's strong front collapsed then, his shoulders slumping and the fight going out of his voice as everything he'd been damming back washed over him at once, leaving him more defeated than pissed. "I really need a win right here."

"Clearly. You hit a bump in the road and start torturing animals?" Todd asked. Jimmy pulled his goggles off, hanging his head. "I mean, what are you gonna do to that little guy?" Jimmy looked down at said little guy, who looked back at him with its round black eyes. "Jimmy, dude, you're better than this, man. Please put that massive syringe down."

I could, Jimmy thought, looking across the kitchen at Todd, who went on, "This is weird, Jimmy. Let's just get out of the house and grab a beer and talk or whatever. Just…c'mon. Stop."

Raising the jar, Jimmy took another look at the frog inside, who let out a plaintive croak as if imploring him to listen to Todd. And for a moment, as he looked back to Todd, who said quietly, "Jimmy," it seemed, for a moment, like he might. Might let the frog go with a story to tell its buddies back in the bushes, might hit one of the bars with Todd that they'd used to close down every night until things got all screwed up and actually let out some of the shit he'd been carrying around with him since Todd had started his mutation from best friend to superior stranger so Todd could tell him he had to grow up, had to change, that chapters end, as he had when he'd announced he was moving out early ("All right, chapters end, but who says this one has to end *now*?" Jimmy had demanded in shock, and Todd hadn't bothered to answer, just gone to start packing up his room).

He turned all this over in his mind, let it spin, and then his small psychopathic smile broke out again and he announced, "I'd rather burn his fucking skin off."

There was a burst of blood in the jar as he squirted the contents of the syringe into it, staring straight at Todd and smirking, the frog disappearing in the swell of scarlet fluid. Almost as satisfying as the kill itself was the look on Todd's face as he said, "I'm done, dude. Grow up."

"Fuck you!" Jimmy shouted after him as he headed back the way he'd come. "I'm a Neanderthal learning how to get out of the trees!" He raised the jar to eye level, directing his next proclamation to its gruesome contents. "Evolve or die, motherfucker!" The laughter burst from him as the blood had burst from the frog, hot and wild. "*YEEEEAAAAHHHH!*"

Music blared through his headphones as he busted through the back door into the blaze of the porch light, hefted the green-and-yellow Super-Soaker in his yellow-gloved hands—"When the hell are you ever gonna use that, Jimmy?" Todd had demanded the day he'd come back from Walmart with it instead of whatever boring shit he'd been sent there for; well, didn't he look like a fucking moron *now*?—and strode into the yard. Giving the water gun a few good pumps he aimed out across the lawn, where the survivors of his first attack were calling to each other, and squeezed the trigger, sending a stream of his personal chemical weapon into their midst with another triumphant whoop. He couldn't let any of them escape this time, and it was only when he was sure he'd coated the whole yard that he lowered the Super-Soaker and pulled his headphones off, waiting.

Nothing. He stood there a few moments more to make sure, but the only sound that reached him was the faint wisp of music still coming from his headphones.

He'd done it. He'd finally silenced the frogs. A wide smile broke on his face, and pulling out the PawPaw's bottle he'd shoved into the pocket of his pants he raised it high, toasting his fallen foes, and drained it in a few long, deep gulps before tossing the empty out into the dark, silent yard and heading back inside.

He figured he'd know if he'd gotten any of the chemicals on him but hopped in the shower to be sure, once he was clean and dry pulling on a fresh pair of shorts and his neon-pink FLY GUY tank top—the humanoid fly on the front seemed pretty pleased with himself, two of his arms wrapped around a couple of busty blonde bare-titted chicks

who seemed equally into him, but there was no way in hell he felt as satisfied as Jimmy did as he flopped into bed, folded his arms behind his head, and for the first night in forever soaked up the silence he'd brought about.

Maybe he could patent this shit, sell it by the gallon—he couldn't be the only guy out there in search of a little peace and quiet. Sure, it was chock-full of toxic chemicals, but if all those class-action lawsuit commercials he always saw on TV were any indication, what *wasn't*?

He'd go online, do some research in the morning, start making calls. If he was lucky, and he was feeling pretty lucky at the moment, he'd make millions off this mix, enough that he wouldn't have to worry about finding another job working for another Bob, or starting the hunt for a new roommate to help pay the bills.

It needed a good name, though. *Frog-Away? Frog Off? Jimmy's Frog-Dissolver... No, DR. Jimmy's Frog-Dissolver, "Dr." always sounds better...*

He was already dreaming as he drifted off to sleep, too

enthralled by his forthcoming fame and fortune to catch the quiet sounds coming from the kitchen he hadn't bothered to clean up before crashing: the soft gurgle of a few bubbles breaking the surface of the bloody fluid in the plastic jar, the low splash of a small hand shooting out of the ooze, green-black and webbed.

He *did* hear the muffled clatter of something falling in the other room, though, and jolted upright, heart beating hard as he sat looking and listening in the darkness.

"Todd, is that you?" he called. Maybe there was something he'd forgotten to pack, or this was some PETA attempt to spring the test-frog….

But the only reply was another muffled thump, the sound of something moving or being moved—the kitchen or living room, he thought, and called again, a small uncertain shake in his voice because if it was Todd, *why wasn't he answering*?, "Real… Real fucking funny."

Still nothing, and *fuck*, he had to get out of bed and look, so he did, walking slowly down the hall, its dimness broken only by the string lights glowing softly on the wall, to the kitchen, looking through its open span into the shadow-soaked living room. It seemed empty, but there still could be some creep hiding behind the couch or in the foyer, so he picked up a knife from the kitchen island as he passed, calling "Todd? You got—You got me," focus fixed on the living room he was heading into, missing the new mess among the one he'd left: the jar overturned, lid off and a trail of wet streaks, scarlet but almost black in the darkness, left across the island, down the drawer, and onto the floor.

There was no more sound of movement, no sign of another person's presence as Jimmy worked his way through the house, room to room, grip tight and sweat-slicked on the handle of the knife, but he couldn't help holding his breath as he approached the door, a white ghost in the gloom, and peered through a slat in the blinds over its small window. "Todd," he said again, quietly, but there was nothing and nobody outside, either, and as he turned away and started back the way he'd come, just as slowly, he started to let himself think there never *had* been anything or anyone in the house; some of the dishes piled in the sink could've shifted, or the broom might've fallen over wherever the hell he'd left it, or…

He stopped because he was back in the hall and there was some kind of green slime splashed along the hallway wall to his left in torso-high smears, slick stains he was definitely, positively, almost certainly sure hadn't been there before.

What the fuck…?

He rubbed his hand tentatively through the stains, which were as slimy to the touch as they looked, slowly drawing his sticky fingers back and studying them in confused disgust, all thoughts of any possible intruder forgotten until a sound of movement came off to his right and he swung his gaze that way, starting with a gasp as the figure stepped out of the shadows.

It was the frog.

Or at least once had been; it was a struggle for Jimmy's frozen brain to reconcile the monster before him with the garden-variety hopper he'd scooped up in the yard earlier. *That* one had looked like the ceramic figures his Nana had collected, cutesy harmless things cluttering up her house; *this* thing was fucking prehistoric, heavy ridges running along its pebbled dark-green skin and a pink cave of an open mouth crammed with small sharp teeth, like the piranhas he'd seen in a nature documentary he'd thought it was a good idea to watch when he was high and which had given him nightmares for weeks afterward.

Nothing in those nightmares could compare to the creature at the end of the hall, though, which straightened as Jimmy stared, horrorstricken—it was tall enough now, standing on two legs, to look him in the eye with its own cold, round, black ones as it took several lumbering steps toward him, the bulk of its body blocking the hall behind it. When it was close enough it raised its hand—because it had a hand now, no webbed thing meant for splashing in ponds but unnervingly long, green, knobby fingers—and touched Jimmy's face for a moment, hot, acrid breath rolling heavily from its glistening mouth.

He still had the knife, and at that leathery touch something broke free in Jimmy's brain, primal instinct driving his hand down and the blade into the creature's arm in a swift sharp jab, like he was trying to pop a balloon with a pin, and sending him bolting down the other end of the hall as it bellowed in pain. As he ran he was aware, in the part of him not screaming that this was not happening, this was fucking impossible, this was FUCKING IMPOSSIBLE, of something long and pink shooting down the hall as well, but it wasn't until he whipped around the corner and saw the tip of it hit, in his peripheral vision, the closet door at the end of the hall that he realized, his internal scream ratcheting up another few decibels, it was the creature's tongue.

He didn't have much time to process this before skidding on something soft and bright yellow-green lying on the threshold of the hall and crashing to the floor, face pressed to the blue carpet and foot twisted in—*fuck*, his hoodie, one of the scattered piles of dirty laundry he'd been meaning to dump into the hamper. *"You're gonna trip on this shit and kill yourself someday, Jimmy,"* his mother berated him in the back of his mind, the memory bursting through his panic in tandem with the pain of impact.

The knife flew out of his hand when he fell, and Jimmy shoved his hair out of his eyes and glimpsed it glinting a few feet away on the floor; he scrambled, strained for it, but the tongue was there, sealing itself to his left hand, pulling it backward into the frog's monstrous mouth as Jimmy cried out in mingled fear and pain. There was a growl no frog had ever, should ever, make and then a hideous crunching as the creature bit, chewed, blinding pain burning in Jimmy's trapped limb and another scream torn from his throat, louder and more ragged than the first.

In the midst of the red haze of pain instinct kicked in again, Jimmy bringing his free hand up in a fist and punching the creature in the face. The mouth opened, teeth releasing his savaged arm, and as the creature moved off Jimmy raised his hand and found the last two fingers of his left hand missing, jagged spars of bright white bone sticking out through the torn and bloody flesh and every pump of his pulse bringing a fresh wave of agony to the wounds.

No time to scream again, though; he had to get out of the house, away from this thing, and when he was somewhere safe he could scream his fucking head off—was *going* to scream his fucking head off, probably for the rest of his life. But first, he had to get his ass moving.

Tucking his wounded arm under his good one, the blood already soaking warm and wet into his shirt, and breathing heavily Jimmy heaved himself to his feet and checked the hall: no sign of the creature, so he made for the back of the house, stumbling through the screen door into the night. *Keep going, almost there, just keep going, keep…*

Shadows were shifting in the yard, growing up from the grass, and as they moved into the glare of the porch light his mouth went dry even as fresh sweat broke on his skin, shock bringing him to a sudden halt. Long, wrinkled, green fingers curled over the wooden beams of the railing; round ridged heads with black-orb eyes and razor-keen teeth rose around him, all of them uttering that *sound*, that hideous growling croak.

"*No*," Jimmy said, and then, more brokenly, "No."

He felt its breath, hot and bitter, on the back of his neck and slowly turned, only for the creature to shove him with inhuman strength against the wall, emitting what was horribly but undeniably a guttural laugh as he raised the Super-Soaker, the remnants of Dr. Jimmy's Frog-Dissolver sloshing in its plastic stomach.

He realized what was about to happen a split second before the mutated frog, still laughing, shoved the nozzle into his mouth and shot a stream of the chemical concoction down his throat, streams of it dribbling down his chin and setting his skin sizzling as Jimmy jerked and gurgled in the frog's grip, searing agony cutting through his spasming body with a

lava-hot blade. When the frog pulled the nozzle free it let Jimmy collapse to the grass, groaning and vomiting slick thick clots of jelly-like blood and God only knew what else as the creature chuckled, tossing the Super-Soaker away after shaking it a bit to make sure it was empty and watching as Jimmy tried to crawl away, mutilated hand still clutched to his body like a bird's wounded wing.

"No..." he moaned weakly, stunned he could manage any sound at all, as the creature advanced off the porch toward him. "No...please..."

Call for help, instinct urged, but there was nobody to hear. Todd would've once, but Todd was gone and he was alone—Todd had left him and he was alone, bleeding and burning inside and, above all else, so goddamn *alone*, and he had no idea how the pain of that could make it through the physical agony savaging him but there it was, unmistakable.

The grass rake was still lying where he'd left it after the first slaughter and he dragged himself toward it, dim desperate hope, but his tormenter reached down and lifted it easily before he could get there, Jimmy rolling onto his back—fresh tongues of fire shooting through his ravaged innards—and holding his uninjured hand up—to shield himself, as an appeal for mercy; even he wasn't sure.

"No, no, no, please, please let me go..."

The frog brought the grass whip up, ignoring his plea as he'd once ignored its, and then, with a croak more akin to a roar, down, once, again, again and again and again, until Jimmy's burbles subsided and his thrashing body grew still in the gore-soaked grass, open eyes staring emptily up at the full moon overhead from a naked face of bone and blood, not hearing the frog's croaking roar echo through the yard and up to the black night sky in triumph.

He didn't feel it as the creatures he'd created descended to feast, one dropping an eyeball into its gaping mouth like a Roman emperor enjoying a plump grape, another gnawing on a severed arm, tearing fat chunks of flesh from the bone, while another of its brothers, bloody intestines dangling from its fang-filled mouth, picked up the fallen Super-Soaker.

Didn't see them heading up the porch steps, peering in through the screen door, pushing it open and moving into the house.

Didn't see them clustered in the kitchen, picking up containers, gazing into a tall beaker full of a familiar frothing green mixture, a pink tongue shooting out to catch a stray fly unlucky enough to be buzzing around the chemical clutter.

Didn't see the massive clutch of translucent, gel-like eggs laid in the darkness, the small murky forms of tadpoles twitching within, eager to escape.

Didn't hear the first of the new brood as, wiggling its tail, testing it out, it raised its head, opened a mouth full of sharp, tiny teeth, and gave a soft croak.

Sarah Cannavo is a writer of prose and poetry haunting southern New Jersey. Her poems and short stories have appeared in anthologies and magazines such as *Liminality*, *Star*Line*, *Pulp Modern*, DBND, Publishing's *Halloween Horror Volume 3*, and *JOURN-E*. Her poems "Fallen But Not Down" and "Learning the Way" were nominated for a 2020 and 2021 Rhysling Award, respectively, and her poem "There Goes the Security Deposit" was nominated for the 2022 Dwarf Stars Award. Her story "Unreality" and her novella *Wolf of the Pines* are now on Amazon. Her website is moodilymusing.blogspot.com.

ASHLEY
UNDERCUFFLER

KEVIN
CALIBER

FELISSA
ROSE

RACHEL
AMANDA BRYANT

XAVIER
ROE

CRAVING

But if you do have that fire in you, if you know that this is the thing you want to give yourself to, then do it.

Matt Barrett
Interview

Matt Barrett directed the short film Croak, featured in *Pulp Modern: Hand of Doom.* He is also a special make up effects artist. We thought it would be interesting to sit down and talk with Matt about his work.

PM: Matt, can you tell us how you got started in makeup and special effects?

MB: I've always loved creatures, stories, and physical art. But in 2001, as the credits rolled on *The Fellowship of the Ring*, all of it fused into a singular, burning passion for movies.

By nineteen, I'd dabbled in effects makeup for Halloween, friends' school projects, movie premiere costumes, etc. But when I moved to Wilmington, NC, for film school, I solely intended to pursue writing and directing my own projects. It did not take long, surrounded by a group of twenty other aspiring writer/directors, to realize that I wasn't as unique as I'd thought. I would need another edge—a different path to get myself plugged into the film industry. That earlier dabbling suggested a potential knack, and so I leaned in.

It started as a strategic move and blossomed into the discovery of a new passion. And it has been quite a ride since then. I now work at Bearded Skulls MUFX Group, the premier makeup effects

shop in North Carolina. And I continue my indie efforts under the banner of Gillybear Films (to which *Croak* belongs). Every day is a new and exciting puzzle. And though I've started going gray earlier than I'd like, I'm thankful all the time to be on this path.

PM: Can you tell us about some of the projects you've worked on, what challenges they presented, and how you went about dealing with those challenges?

MB: After years of music videos, student shorts, and very, very indie features, my first "oh I've heard of that one" movie was *The Black Phone*. This was also my official introduction to the Bearded Skulls, helping them in applying the ghostly look to The Grabber's earlier victims, and a few other things here and there.

From then til now, the primary challenges have always been the same, regardless of the scale of production: time and money. There's often not enough of both of them at the same time. Mix in an occasional last-minute creative change from on high, and you've got all the elements for some stormy sailing.

Speaking of boats, a recent example: *The Waterfront* on Netflix. While not in the horror genre, it's a crime thriller that still has its share of simulated bodily trauma. Our fingerprints were all over that one, stretching from makeup and makeup effects into props. I can't list everything because, you know, spoilers. But one order required us to churn out about 250 realistic foam fish for one of the sets. This is while there are still other bodies to make, and new orders for additional stunt-safe props continuing to come in. There were long hours (it was such a blur that we later forgot some of the things we'd made in that period).

You deal with it by looking your team in the eye, agreeing "this is gonna take some work, but we're going to pull it off", and then buckling down and doing it. When you hit the finish line, the director and producers are happy, and you get to celebrate for a moment

until the next wave comes. Nothing beats that feeling.

PM: Let's talk about *Croak*. Where did the idea come from, and how did you go about bringing it to life?

MB: Back in my college era, while I was working to gain a reputation among my peers as someone who could take trash and turn it fantastical, I made a list of different effects I'd wanted to shoot for a reel. Not fully fleshed out narratives, just enough to show people what I could offer them. There was one in particular that stuck with me—a giant, slimy creature looming over a guy and touching his face (physical interaction between things always adds to the sensation of reality). But it would take a few months and some "life events" for that slimy seed to get frog-flavored and flesh out into a story.

Around this time, I existed pretty exclusively in two modes. If I wasn't holed up in my room mixing various chemicals for effects research, then I was partying with my roommates. There were five of us altogether, and we were always getting into something. Downtown debauchery, late-night conversation catharsis, and more than a few "I hope we survive for this to become a funny story" moments. All the classics.

After about a year and a half, one of them had enough of the college boy lifestyle and decided it was time for him to move out. I think you might see where I'm going with this.

The characters Jimmy and Todd are not any specific guys in that gang of roommates, but sort of a distillation and dramatization of our collective experience. The story was born out of the ending of this era, and my reckoning with the idea of the "party being over, dude". Jimmy is angry about this, but he's heartbroken too. He found meaning in that era of his life, and is afraid of what things look like after it. He just hap-pens to turn those feelings in the wrong direction, and things go... poorly.

The roommates and I actually started shooting an early version of *Croak*, but it never got completed (my partner Delanie Gilliss, the "Gilly" part of Gillybear Films, has a very fun idea for how to use that footage in the future. Hint: Dramatic Reenactment).

About a year later, my friend and fellow filmmaker Ben Pellington floated the idea of making a short film together and asked if I had any ideas. I told him about the deadbeat party-boy who goes to war with the frogs, and $400 and a lot of favors later, we had a fun little cartoon-horror short.

PM: In addition to the creatures in *Croak*, what make up creations of yours are you most proud of and why?

MB: There have been many exciting things—an animatronic gremlin for Netflix, a ten-foot realistic marlin, countless dead bodies, and more. But the work I'm proudest of so far was entirely outside of the film industry.

In 2023, with work slowed due to the strikes, we had the time and opportunity to point our talents down a different dark alley—the haunted attraction business. We formed Port City Fear Factory and began designing our first event, "Chapel of Horrors".

Rather than simply being a series of random horror vignettes, Chapel of Horrors was designed to be an immersive experience. From your "character's" per-spective, you might not detect every bit of lore. But you could tell that there was a rea-son all of this was happening, and that you've stumbled into something bigger than you ought not to have messed with.

I came up with the core concept and characters and wrote chapters of optional backstory for people to follow along in advance of the event. Together, we made all the props, costumes, mechanical gags, and creatures. And the rest was just like a movie—our friends from other departments helped us with cinematic lights and detailed set design.

Everything created for Chapel of Horrors was custom-made and entirely ours. No off-the-shelf Halloween masks, no design notes from a room of producers, completely ours. And I think we came up with some very enticingly sinister stuff. *Fangoria* even featured one creature I partilarly love (an exoskeletal nightmare called a "Kalmutu") on their Instagram page!

It was all extremely fulfilling, strongly scratching both my "creature making" and "world-building" urges. And the desire to entertain as well—I still smile when I think about the range of emotions I saw on those security monitors. For all the odds we battled against to pull it off, it was worth it in those moments.

PM: You've done work for both independent and 'mainstream' projects. What differences have you found working in both arenas?

Well, there is the obvious one. Indies are acts of love, but mainstream keeps the lights on.

But it's more than just a difference in pay rate. That contrast in budget also impacts how things are done. Something mainstream will have more money to throw towards a solution, whereas indie is often "this is all we've got, we've got to make it work".

People often transition from indie to mainstream and never look back. But to me, it's important to always keep a foot in both worlds. I see those financial limitations as a challenge, an opportunity to keep the crafty parts of the mind active and in shape.

At the end of the day, I love them both for different reasons, and I love it when they cross-pollinate. One thing is consistent in both worlds: the sense of camaraderie. Your crew members are your teammates, and you're all working together to make something that will excite and entertain. A foot in both worlds furthers that sense

of unity, to the benefit of all.

PM: What advice would you have for younger filmmakers looking to work in your field?

MB: The very first thing I'd say is this: You need to love it. Or you need to think that you could fall in love with it. Because I will tell you right now, even as someone who is starting to become the version of themselves that they'd dreamed of, this is not easy. There are very long hours, tight deadlines, high expectations, and dangerous chemicals. And that's just on the special effects end of this answer; the filmmaking side can feel even more daunting (and doesn't come with a paycheck for a long time).

But if you do have that fire in you, if you know that this is the thing you want to give yourself to, then do it.

Be realistic about your expectations, use what you have access to, and make something. If you hate it, then learn from it and make the next thing better. Eventually, the end product will get closer to what you pictured. The important part is to keep making things. I unfortunately know people who theoretically could have been great writers, directors, or makeup effects artists, but they didn't get past the "this sucks, I hate it" phase and stopped. I'm no master of any of these things, and still feel plenty of "this didn't turn out as well as I'd pictured it." But I know what moves me, and so I keep going.

Here's the thing—no one in this entire world is going to fight for your art more than you, and it's not going to just suddenly happen one day without that fight. But if you feel the drive to make monsters or tell stories, you already know right it feels when you're doing it. You don't need me to tell you that. What you may need to hear is this: your art is possible, even without $10,000 for an industry-standard monster suit.

That man-sized mutant toad in *Croak*? Cotton balls, craft store latex (half-off with a coupon), and upholstery foam from a dumpster. That Kalmutu on *Fangoria*'s Instagram? Pretty much the same thing.

The shot is the final product. You're painting an image in the audience's mind. Be creative, resourceful, and plan those shots accordingly. You can find a way. You know you've got a cool idea. Make it happen so that we can all enjoy it.

Encouraging others who want to do this is an important part of my core mission, so I have a lot of thoughts here. But rather than eating up further big chunks of your magazine, I'll say this—if you're reading this, and you know that I'm talking to you, find me on Instagram and reach out. @MattBarrett777

PM: Finally, Matt, what are you working on these days and what can we look forward to seeing from you in the near future?

MB: I believe, by the time this comes out, you'll be able to see the work we did for *Dexter: Resurrection*. That's a blood-colored feather in the cap that I am extremely proud of, and it remains a surreal moment for me. Younger Matt, early into the spatter-studying, was a big *Dexter* fan.

Beyond that, the haunted house world is about to expand in new and exciting ways (and perhaps I shouldn't have said it was all *entirely* outside of the film industry). And I've got a handful of other personal projects, both the near-future and long-term varieties, that I keep growing at a steady pace.

On that note: conversations have begun regarding one wacky world that has another chapter or two of story left to tell, and I'd love to tell you all about it. It's just... hold on... can someone do something

about that noise? What the hell kind of frogs are...

PM: We can see you need to go take care of that. We look forward to seeing your work on *Dexter*. Thanks for taking the time to talk with us and thanks for your excellent advice for younger filmmakers out there. Good luck with those frogs!

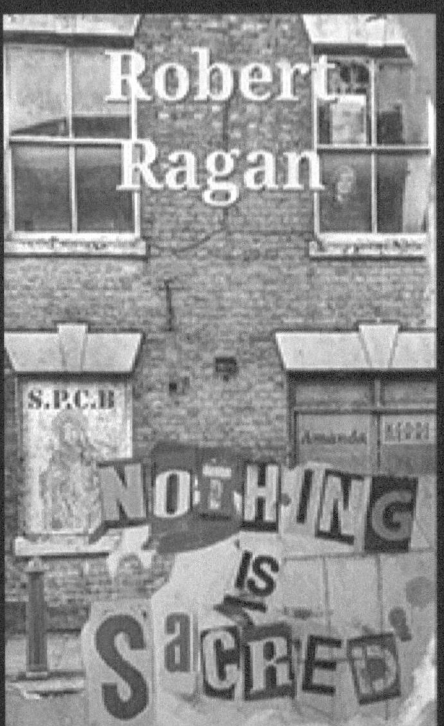

THE
POET
LAUREATE
OF THE
STREETS

UNCLE B.
PUBLICATIONS

WHEREVER GOOD BOOKS ARE SOLD

NOBODY'S COMING HOME

crime fiction stories by
ALEC CIZAK

13 EXERCISES IN MODERN NOIR BY THE MOST CONTROVERSIAL CRIME FICTION WRITER OF THE MODERN AGE

ABC
GROUP DOCUMENTATION

Find
Crime Fiction
and
True Crime
@
THE YARD
theyardcrimeblog.com

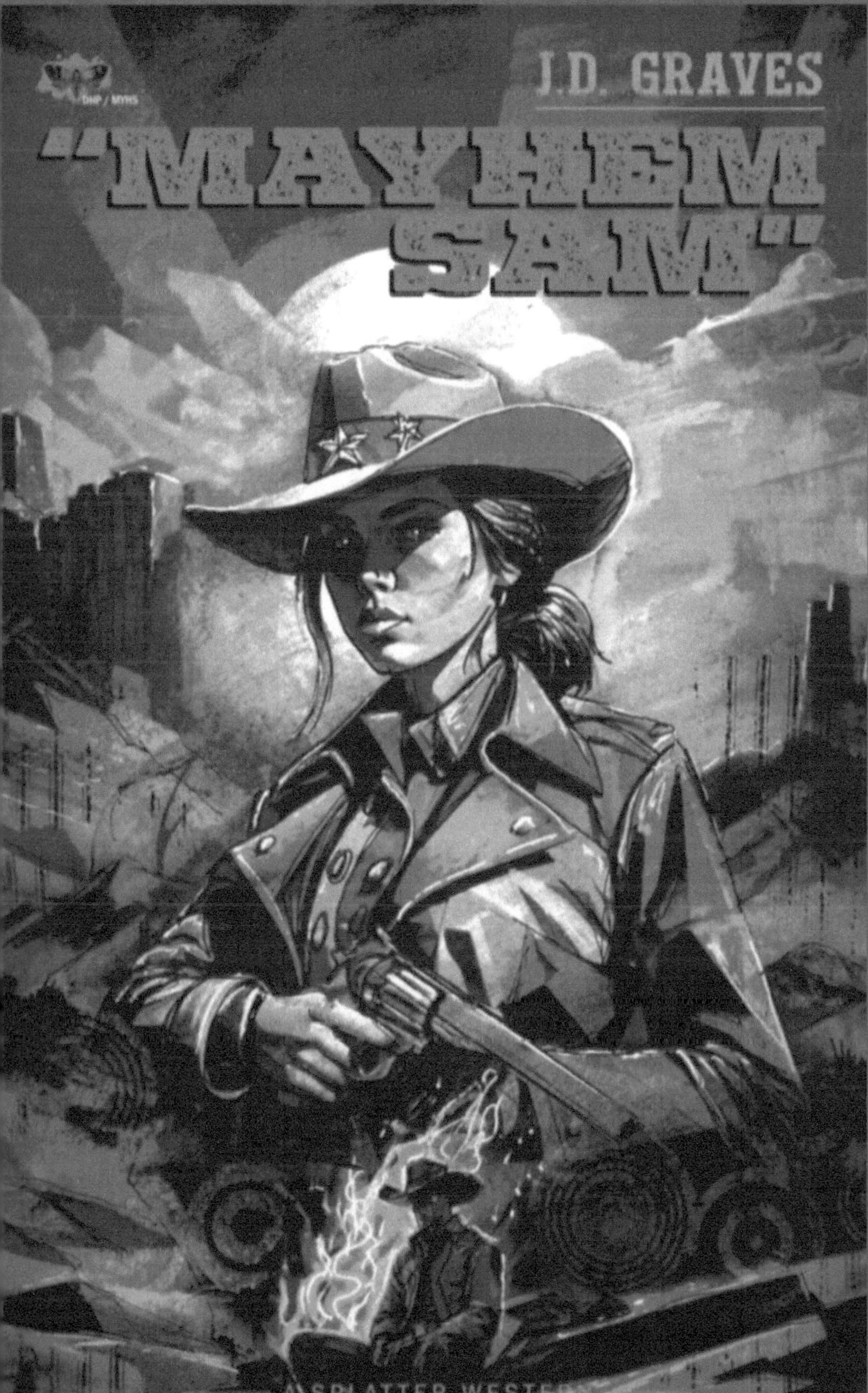
J.D. GRAVES
"MAYHEM SAM"
A SPLATTER WEST

A.B. PATTERSON

JASPER
THE GLOVES ARE OFF

A novella based on the
cult classic film
starring Nathan Hill

ANDREW MILLER

NAMASTE MARTY CONFIDENTIAL

"A wild tale of wannabe private dicks, twisted
religious nuts, psychopathic Armenian gangsters
and crazed celebrity-chasers. Andrew Miller is a
talent to watch."
—Steven Powell
author of *Love Me Fierce in Danger, The Life of James Ellroy*

The
Independent
Fiction
Alliance

Writers and Publishers
Committed to the
Freedom of Speech

www.Independentfictionalliance.com

CLASH BOOKS
presents a novel by
DuVay Knox

Private
Dick on
the Case.

The Pussy Detective

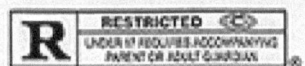
RESTRICTED
UNDER 17 REQUIRES ACCOMPANYING
PARENT OR ADULT GUARDIAN

Harry's
Back!

HARRY'S
GRAIL

A. B. PATTERSON

EXCELLENT
SEQUEL TO
INTERNATIONAL
AWARD-WINNING
NOVEL **HARRY'S**
WORLD
HARRY'S
QUEST

from the
undisupted bad boy
of Australian
crime fiction...
A.B. PATTERSON

OZZY OSBOURNE

1948 - 2025

"I think there's a wild man in everybody.
All I am is a conductor of mayhem."